Aura Leigh

DEANNA RAY

Copyright © 2015 Deanna Brown.

All rights reserved. No part of this book may be reproduced, stored, or transmitted by any means—whether auditory, graphic, mechanical, or electronic—without written permission of both publisher and author, except in the case of brief excerpts used in critical articles and reviews. Unauthorized reproduction of any part of this work is illegal and is punishable by law.

This is a work of fiction. All of the characters, names, incidents, organizations, and dialogue in this novel are either the products of the author's imagination or are used fictitiously.

ISBN: 978-1-4834-3762-0 (sc)
ISBN: 978-1-4834-3761-3 (e)

Because of the dynamic nature of the Internet, any web addresses or links contained in this book may have changed since publication and may no longer be valid. The views expressed in this work are solely those of the author and do not necessarily reflect the views of the publisher, and the publisher hereby disclaims any responsibility for them.

Any people depicted in stock imagery provided by Thinkstock are models, and such images are being used for illustrative purposes only.
Certain stock imagery © Thinkstock.

Lulu Publishing Services rev. date: 09/11/2015

Acknowledgment

The author wishes to make grateful acknowledgement to the following people:

To my wonderful daughters, April, Crystal, and Amanda. You all are so special to me. I could not have ordered more wonderful children who have grown to become strong women with kind and generous hearts! I am so proud of each of you and love you so.

April, thank you for proofreading my manuscript, each section diligently, editing at home, and with me, assisting and offering suggestions. To Crystal and Amanda who read and critiqued each chapter with motivation and love.

To my dear, best friend Debbie for listening to each chapter via telephone, who also read and gave monetary support to help get this process going and the many suggestions you have offered through the years. Thank you so much for finding me after many years apart, and thank you for not giving up on me.

To my precious friend Geri who sat on the floor with me, going over my book and offering ideas and being so positive and patient with a listening and loving ear. Throughout this journey, you have been here.

To my sister Judy and niece Melody, who encouraged and offered support during the writing of my book. You believed in me and my ability to write this book and that meant so much.

In loving memory of my cousin Wanda who listened, read and offered advice and support during the writing of the book-I miss and love you so much.

To my beautiful brown eyed cousin Fayrene for your positive encouragement as you read and offered support, through the years. You believed in me and that meant so much.

To Nancy whose tireless enthusiasm for the book and wisdom, support and assistance was and is so appreciated.

To Donna, Linda, Vicki, Jennifer, and Kerith, and Doug for their interest and positive words when reading the manuscript. To all of my friends at work and friends outside of work who took home manuscripts and offered their support, their time and thoughts during the making of my book.

A huge thank you to Stephanie Felsinger, the beautiful and graceful model for the book cover. I knew you were my heroine the first time I saw you. Special thanks to Robin for capturing your essence on camera.

To Tashia Shamwell – graphic designer. You designed the beautiful cover of my book with professionalism and style. Your help and expertise through this journey is most appreciated. To Duncan Chaboudy for the audio recording of the first draft of the book.

I would like to offer a special thank you to Hamilton for taking the time from your busy schedule to read and help edit my book. What a wonderful teacher and mentor you are. You gave hope to a girl who had no belief in herself. Always grateful am I.

To my handsome dad; without you I would not be here. I love you.

And now a very special thank you:

In memory of my dear, beautiful mother who worked tirelessly to raise me. She taught me strength, morality and love. She was a mother and my friend. I miss talking to you, visiting with you and grocery shopping with you. What a great cook and strong woman you were. I miss your smell and just sitting beside you. I will miss you and love you always and always.

Chapter One

It was the spring of 1935. I awoke to the sun streaming through the starched white curtains, crossing the room where it lay across my bed. I wasn't big at all, small really. I had olive skin and dark brown hair, just like my eight sisters and one brother. I guess you could say that we had a full house.

While lying in the large feather bed with a sister on each side of me, I wriggled free for something smelled really good coming up from the kitchen. I climbed over a pair of legs and jumped to the cool wooden floor. I quickly dressed not even caring that the noise I was making caused the other girls to wake. "Let us sleep!" snapped one of the sisters. After a moment, the heavy quilts began moving and the girls stretched and started getting out of bed. Night gowns were being pulled off over their heads as they began getting dressed. While buttoning their dresses, the girls gathered by the round dresser mirror. One would nudge the others' shoulders in an attempt to see themselves. Then the hair brushing began. You had to look presentable at the table.

As the girls were finishing up, I was already dressed and certainly not waiting. I ran past each of the girls, out of the room and to the wooden staircase. I held on to the railing as I quickly raced down the big steps. I was the first to arrive to the kitchen and slowed down a bit as I walked in.

Mama didn't allow us youngins to run through the house like we were high idiots. That was just one of the many terms I never really stopped to figure out. I just knew it was meant for me to slow down and walk. When I got to the table, I climbed up into the large, wooden chair. What a smile must have crossed my face as I peered at a meal fit for a king. Well, there was no king, just my sisters, brother, Mama and daddy all sitting down to this feast of a meal. Homemade buttermilk biscuits were steaming from a large bowl. There was rich, brown gravy with a ladle for dipping. Piles of country ham lay abundantly on a huge platter. As I continued to look, there were mounds of scrambled eggs and fried potatoes, sliced in circles and browned with bacon grease. Mama saved the bacon grease and kept it on the stove to cook with. I thought it made the food taste extra special. I wiggled with delight in my chair.

I was almost five years old. It was hard for me to sit still while Daddy prayed. Devout as he was, he'd ask us to bow our heads as he prayed and prayed and prayed. He went on forever! I just knew the food would be cold by the time he got through. It was all I could do to be still with my eyes closed. Truth be known, I had one eye closed. I used the other to peer around the table and see if everyone else had their eyes closed. Finally, we could start passing this wonderful breakfast around our table. They didn't think I could pick up the heavy bowls though I was sure I could. Mama would fix mine and Leannas' plate because we were the youngest. I was in Heaven as I ate my soft buttermilk biscuit with mounds of gravy swirling deliciously around my tongue! The room was full of talk about the coming day's events. Now if I had a choice of eating or talking, it would seem like words were just a waste of time. Especially when it came to enjoying my Mamas' cooking….

After breakfast, the large white house was alive with business inside and out. Leftover food was scraped from the heavy, rose pattern plates and into a large bowl for the pigs. All you had to do was pour the food into their long, wooden trough and the pigs went to snorting up their food. They loved Mama's cooking too. It wasn't long until that trough was licked plum clean.

Everyone knew they had a job to do. With hot water heated on the coal stove, one girl washed dishes in the metal dish pan. Another pan would be used to rinse. Each dish was then dried perfectly. What a pretty shine the dishes had as they were placed neatly into the cupboard. The red and white checked linoleum floor was always swept neatly after each meal. Not that the floor was ever dirty. I just think dirt would be afraid to fall onto our floor in the first place. My Godly mother just wouldn't allow it.

Over by the door was my older sister Gayetta. She had dark, wavy hair that flowed gently about her small shoulders. She put on a white apron and tied the bow neatly in the back. This always amazed me when she couldn't even see what she was doing. Yet each and every time the bow was neat and centered. She was getting herself ready for her daily chores. She always started with milking our cow. Out through the screen door she went. The door kind of creaked when it opened and then slammed loudly. After a couple steps, she was out into our back yard.

Behind the house, Gayetta walked on up the hillside and towards the pasture. Once there, she became a dark silhouette. What a beautiful outline of her slender frame against the morning sky. As the sun began gently rising, she led the cow slowly to the red barn.

Reaching for the oil lantern on a shelf by the door, Gayetta struck a match. The blue and yellow flame touched the wick and the room illuminated with light. A faded wooden ladder to the loft was just ahead. To the right there was a large amount of hay piled high and resting in the corner. The smell of the fresh cut hay was abundant in this large barn. She retrieved the metal pail from the barn wall, which was hanging securely on a rusty nail. Pulling an old milk stool from the corner of the barn, she sat upon it readying herself to milk the cow.

The large brown and white cow was seen clearly by the flickering light. The cow had a white face and large, soulful, brown eyes. Old Betsy was the cow's name. Betsy really didn't like to give up her milk. More than one of the sisters had encountered a swat from Old Betsy's white tail. Only

Gayetta had the knack to calm Betsy as she would sit patiently by. Soon warm fresh milk flowed into the metal pail.

Thinking back… There was a very sad time not so long ago. Daddy had sold Betsy's baby calf to a neighbor down the road. That little calf was always by her Mama's side. Betsy was forever using that tongue of hers as she gave her baby a bath. Every morning Betsy would chew the grass that seemed to grow a little higher by the fence line. The baby calf stood faithfully by. What great company they must have been for each other on those long summer days.

One morning, there came a truck to the farm. Daddy and another man loaded the baby into the truck. What crying was heard! The baby had high pitched noises which came out of her mouth as Old Betsy's moo deepened in a loud, threatened way. Over and over Betsy cried out as if to say, "Don't take my baby!" Deep inside, she knew there was nothing she could do. The crying went on for days. Daddy said Betsy would get along and quit this nonsense by the end of the week. He was right. Each day she cried a little less until she finally cried no more. She was resolutely alone. Emptiness remained in those large brown eyes. I knew it was because she missed her baby.

Back to the mornings' events: In the house my sister Audrey and Mama were finishing cleaning the kitchen. The coal stove gleamed from all the shining Mama gave it. The slats beneath the beds never saw a speck of dust. Cleanliness was next to Godliness my Mama used to say and I knew that this was true.

I believe the local preacher of our church knew how close Mama was to God and that was why he would come eat with us after church on Sundays. He, like Daddy, was also long winded when he talked to God or about God. How many Sundays I would try to count the dots on the ceiling while he preached and prayed. Women would kneel by the pews and pray and cry and I'd just keep on counting. Thinking back I wonder how far I could count. Must not have been much for I wasn't even five. I probably made up numbers just to pass the time.

They tell me Daddy and some of the neighbors built this house from scratch. This seemed amazing to me! We had fireplaces in all the bedrooms as well as the living room. It was a two story, white, clapboard house with green shutters and a gray, wrap around porch. On rainy nights, the tin roof of our house made sleeping quite a pleasure. We had no electricity, just light from the oil lamps would cast an iridescent glow throughout the polished house that I called home.

They say Daddy fell from a ladder when finishing up the place. He was painting the side of the house, lost his footing and fell down to the grass. He hit the back of his head on a jagged rock that was protruding through the grass. White paint spilled and soon mixed with a bright red oozing from Daddy's head. Mama yelled for a cold, wet rag. Mama wiped his brow and held the rag firmly to the bleeding wound. Daddy didn't move for a minute or so. Mama said that was the longest minute of her life. Finally, the bleeding slowed and he came around. He slowly got up to his feet, but never was his strong self after that. He kept working to support the family. He was a conductor on the railroad. Well heck, nearly every man I knew either worked in the coal mines or on the railroad, not to mention having a big farm to tend. That's just the way it was.

Daddy was a tall handsome man with dark hair. He had somewhat of a temper and the fear of God at the same time. If he wanted something done, of course it was done.... Henry (my only brother) was Daddy's right hand man. Whenever Daddy wasn't at work, they were always out on the tractor, plowing the field, hoeing the garden, or working in the barn. There was always something that needed fixing and nothing was left undone.

Henry was eighteen years old, tall like Daddy and trim. He had brown hair and a strong, smooth face. He was a quiet sort of man with a slow, easy smile. It seems like he picked at me more than the other sisters and I sure liked it. We just got along. I wanted to grow up and marry a man as handsome and sweet as my brother.

Often, after a hard day's work, Henry would take me out and lead the ole brown horse and let me ride. We'd go down the old dirt road and turn up the hillside. My brother would then let the reins go and the horse would be running all over those hills... it would be all I could to stay on. So scary, yet so exciting! When the riding was done, I'd wrap my arms securely about Henry's neck. He'd gently let me down to the ground. I'd hold on tightly and get such a nice hug from him. This is a memory I will never forget.

Henry soon left home to marry his longtime girl Patty Sue. She was a pretty girl with a ready smile, kind of short and full figured. She was just the kind of girl you couldn't help but like, even if she did take my brother from home.

Henry worked the coal mines to care for his sweet bride. More than once I'd go visit my brother and stay all night. He'd come home with so much coal dust on him, the only thing you could see were the whites of his eyes. He'd take his coveralls off outside the door and put them in a box. Shoes too, for everywhere he walked, coal dust would follow. Patty Sue would have his water heated and poured into a big, metal tub that stayed on her screened back porch. I'd go inside and wait while Henry scrubbed and scrubbed to get all that dirt off. Patty Sue would stay out there and help Henry with his bath. You could hear them laugh and laugh. It made bathing sound like lots of fun! They sure did get along well. Never a harsh word did I ever hear my brother say to Patty and she was always smiling at him.

On what seemed to be an ordinary day, I helped Patty do her daily chores. Towards evening, there came a knock on the door. I was in the kitchen as Patty opened the door. I heard a man's voice that I had never heard before. All of a sudden Patty yelled "Come on!" to me, which scared me. The time I have known Patty, she has never raised her voice to anyone. We got in the strangers car and I sat in the back. The ride had an eerie silence which was unsettling to my spirit. I felt something terrible had happened, though I was afraid to ask.

A large crowd was gathered at the mines as we pulled in. Sobs from women crying became louder as we approached. We were told that they tried the best they could; however, they could not get to the miners. A large roof fall had taken my brother from me- from all of us. Overwhelmed, tears ran down my face and I could not brush them away fast enough. Patty Sue held me close. I remember looking up at her face. Tears rolled silently down her face and yet, not one sob escaped from her lips. A total of seven miners lost their lives that day.

At home Mama knelt to her knees upon finding out her only son would never be home again. Daddy, on the other hand, appeared stern and quiet. I knew how bad this must have hurt him, because Henry was his only son and they were so close. Even after marrying Patty, Henry still had found time to help Daddy with the chores on weekends. Now Daddy had no one. Well, except us girls.

A large funeral for all the men was held at our tiny church. Pews were full and standing wall to wall were all the people of our town. Each miner had a loved one who said something good about him and then the preacher had a small sermon.

After he prayed for each of the miners souls, we went out to the church's graveyard. There was a designated area for each of the miners with small gravestones. It seemed so odd to have a funeral without a casket. I felt like the miners were just around the corner, that they would soon show their faces and life would get back to normal. Of course that wasn't the case. Little did I know, things would keep changing and would never be the same.

Mama had me stay with Patty after brother Henry passed. Mama said Patty needed the company. As sad as I was, it just didn't seem to compare to Patty's sorrow. She seemed just devastated. She would sit for hours and stare at the wall. I'd have to remind her to eat. She'd nibble a little and then push the plate away. She'd say she just wasn't hungry. After a few weeks Patty began to throw up. I told Mama about it and she got the doctor to come and look at Patty. After checking Patty, a smile spread across the doctor's face. "This is nothing a few more months won't fix." "Patty, you're going to have a baby!" the doctor said. Mama squeezed Patty's hand and then they hugged and cried. What a wonderful change came over the whole room!

Patty's folks had so many children to care for; they just didn't seem to have room for Patty. It just seemed natural for Patty to come and live with us. Mama smiled more as she made baby gowns and booties on her sewing machine. Patty would call out different names for boys and girls. It was a time of healing for us all.

True to Patty's nature, not one scream escaped her lips while she was in labor. Leanna and I had to wait downstairs until the baby came. The doctor finally came down. "It's a boy," he said. We ran quickly up the stairs and slowed a bit when getting to the bedroom door. We knocked as quietly as we could, though we were excited! Mama opened the door. "Look at your nephew, girls," Mama smiled. Cradled in Patty's arms was a small baby with a lot of black hair. "Meet Henry Jr.," Patty said, her eyes brimming with tears. "The Lord has blessed me with a grandson," Mama beamed with pride. We all gathered around and hugged and cried. A bittersweet time to remember...

As the days grew into months, we went about doing our chores. I was lucky I had so many sisters that were older than me. Lottie, Audrey, Gayetta, Dianna, Gayle, and Hannah were all older so they got most of the chores. I was next to the baby. My primary job was to take good care of my sister and to keep her out of trouble. Leanna was the baby. She was named after Mama. What a beautiful little dark haired sister she was! She had a light dusting of freckles across her nose and a genuine smile. She got by with even more than I did. Sometimes this made me mad, but other times I didn't care because I loved her so much.

Daddy never fully recovered from the fall off the ladder. As time rolled on, his headaches just kept getting worse. Nothing eased them. The doctor finally said Daddy should see a specialist in Baltimore. This was something that was hard to imagine. Baltimore, he might as well have been going to the moon!

We didn't have a car. No one did except for the Gregor's. They had plenty of money. I believe they were the only people in town that did. They owned the general store and half the town (which wasn't much). Their car was a large Buick. That thing was a city block long, I am sure of it. It was black and shiny. When walking with Daddy to the store, we strolled by that wonderful car. I just wanted to run my hand along the side of it. I could just imagine the coolness of the metal next to my hand. It was like Daddy knew what I was thinking. He'd say, "Aura Leigh, keep those hands to yourself and don't put them on things that don't belong to you." Of course my hands went right to my sides. I didn't dare go against my Daddy. You just didn't do that sort of thing. I think it was enough anyway just to see such a beautiful car. Eyes are such wonderful things.

They left on a Monday and went by train. It was hard seeing Daddy board the train, for who knew how long he would be gone! Mama went with him. The older sisters took care of the farm with a little help from a neighbor across the way. He would come and check on us from time to time. There just wasn't another alternative.

Two weeks to the day, Mama and Daddy arrived at the train station in Flannery. The wheels of old #6 train came screeching to a halt. Dark smoke billowed high up into the air. I was eager with anticipation for the door to open. After what seemed to be an eternity, people began making their way down the train stairs. My small Mama climbed down from the train first. Then, Daddy followed, holding on tightly to the rails. He seemed to shake as he descended the stairs. Mama quickly took his arm to support him as they began walking toward us.

Oh how I had missed my handsome dark haired daddy! I missed him picking me up and swinging me around the room. I also missed my soft Mama and her buttermilk biscuits. Daddy looked different. He'd lost weight and was pale. Mama looked very tired.

Once we got home, my Daddy no longer picked me up. It was as if his get up and go had got up and gone. He sat around mostly, as I remember and finally he just didn't get up anymore. I'd go to his bed to see my Daddy. He'd tousle my hair and I'd kiss his cheek, ever so careful cause he always complained of a headache. One day I woke up and the house was very quiet except for the soft crying of my Mama. I went and hugged her around her white aproned skirt. I knew something was bad, very bad. My daddy had died.

Chapter Two

No matter how early I awoke, it would never early enough! I'd run to Mama's room, but it was too late. No Mama. She's up and gone before the day begins. The wind had picked up and rain was really pounding on the tin roof of our house. The brooding sky was filled with charcoal gray clouds of various shapes with an occasional flash in the distance.

It must be a hard walk for Mama today. She walks five miles to the sewing factory every day, five days a week. Mama's been working since Daddy passed. I hear the older ones say she had to work so as not to lose the farm. If it bothered her, you'd never know. I have never heard her complain. If she thought bad things, she kept them to herself. She wouldn't let us youngins say anything against anyone, either. Mama would say, "You don't know about a person until you walk in his shoes."

Mama was 45 years old, very pretty, 4 ft 11 inches tall and maybe 100 pounds. Her soft, dark hair was always brushed back and swept up neatly with combs. She wore various hats that matched her dresses when she went into town. She always had a soft, yet determined look about her. She was a Mama to be proud of.

Gayetta was next in line to take care of us youngins. The sisters that were older than her had married and moved out. Gayetta did most of the cooking. Oh, she was quite a cook too. Though her biscuits are soft and good, they just weren't Mama's.

Gayetta was a junior when she had to quit high school. Somebody had to take care of the farm. There was no choice since Daddy's gone. If she was upset about leaving school, she never let on. Sometimes I'd see her watch the other girls with a wistful look on her face. But as soon as it appeared, it was gone and she was back doing her chores.

Upstairs, the skirts were flying about the bedrooms as the girls were getting ready for school. Gail was the tallest. She's slightly larger than the rest of the girls. She had a radiant face with scattered freckles and beautiful smile that was subject to change at the drop of a hat. Sternness often took its place that would make your blood run cold. "Hang that blouse back up if you're not going to wear it! Mama didn't raise us to be heathens," she'd say. I often wondered what a heathen was, but I sure wasn't going to ask Gail. She'd probably say that I was just being a "smart ellic," (ain't quite sure what that was either). She was firm, and it seemed to work. The younger girls did just what Gail said. She was kind of like an assistant to Gayetta in telling us what to do. Yes, she was firm, guess she got that from Daddy.

The next sister was Dianne. Maybe I should put Dianne and Hannah together. Wonder if that would be rude. The thing was, if you saw Dianne, Hanna would be close behind. They were less than one year apart in age, closer than sisters and best friends. They had an understanding about each other that the rest of us did not have. There was never a temper nor a bad word found in either of them. Peaceful and quiet like two fragile flowers, that was what I would say. Little did I know the tragedy that life would bring on these two girls. Dianne and Hannah were very petite along with dark hair and olive skin. They sure were good to me and Leanna. Sometimes when Mama baked cookies, they'd sneak a couple of them from the kitchen when no one was looking. Believe me; you ain't supposed to eat nothing unless you were at the kitchen table!

The clothes were flying, socks on, hair neatly combed on everyone's head, including Leanna's and mine. There was not one bobby pin is out of place. With a girl on each side of the bed, the bed making began. The closets were in order, shirts, skirts, and blouses. After the room was completely finished, then and only then could we go see what Gayetta had prepared for breakfast.

After clearing the table, the girls put their sweaters on and with books in hand they ran out the front door. Walking to school looked like a wonderful adventure as Leanna and I watched the girls go down the long dirt road.

Leanna and I spent the days outside, free to explore. The chickens pecked at their daily ration of corn and settin hens perched quietly on their nest. We would attempt to go near their nest to check and see who had eggs. Hens would begin to squawk and we'd run like there was no tomorrow. I can't imagine what pecking and flogging from a mad hen might feel like and sure didn't want to find out. Like Mama Use to say—madder than an ole wet hen.

Old Betsy was grazing on the lush, green hillside along with Mama's sheep. The clouds seem to hang lazily, right on top of the hillside. This made the deep, green grass seem like it stretched all the way to Heaven! Thinking back it must have been quite a feast for the animals.

What a beautiful day it was! The bright yellow sun spread its warm rays all about our small community and smiled down on Mamas green and lush garden. The juicy red tomatoes hung on the vine and were ready to be picked. Leanna and I would run down the neat rows of hearty staked tomatoes and picked us a large red one. How wonderful it tasted as the flavor burst in your mouth with each bite. You hoped the tomato would stay in your mouth, but often times the seeds would squirt right out and down your chin. We'd laugh and just try to wipe it off as best we could. There were vines of half runner green beans, full and lush. The large stalks of silver queen corn that seem to go on without end. The list of vegetables goes on and on. Each one lined in neat rows.

We also had an apple tree. Those apples sure were sour. As we bit into them, there was always a pucker on our faces. We'd look carefully for worm holes before taking a big bite because there's nothing worse than biting into an old worm. Well, now that I think about it, guess worms have to eat too. Those apples sure made wonderful pies. Momma made many of those, especially on Sundays after church.

On the left side of our home, a tire swing hung securely with thick rope on the old maple tree. What hours of fun we had pushing each other higher and higher into the air. Sometimes you felt as if you were as high as the house. Then there were times when we'd just sit in the tire swing and take turns spinning one another around. You sure couldn't walk straight after jumping down from that swing. Most times you just ended up falling down.

"Leanna, I'm gonna beat you to the barn," I yelled. It wasn't hard to outrun Leanna. She was a year younger and her legs were shorter. "You wait, one day I will pass you up," she said breathlessly. She caught up with me at the barn's door. Inside, the ladder waited for me to climb to the loft. Leanna lay in the straw below. I would make one daring jump after another. It just felt wonderful landing in the soft bed of straw. Leanna just laughed and laughed. After a few daring jumps, we'd lie in the hay and relax. The smell of the fresh straw was abundant as the sunlight filtered through the cracks in the wood.

One evening while up in the loft, I saw a small birds nest. It was built securely in the corner, just within reach. "Wonder if she has any eggs in that nest?" Leanna asked, standing at the foot of the ladder. Me being the older one, I thought I'd check and see. Reaching into the nest, I felt a small, smooth egg. I smiled and started to tell Leanna. However, the smile suddenly changed to terror. For wrapped into a coiling position, a copperhead snake was staring angrily at me! He wanted that egg for himself. This I was sure of. I slowly took steps backward. All the while my eyes fixed on that snake. I talked as peaceful to the snake as I could under the circumstances. "You can have that egg. It will taste good Mr. Snake. It's all yours." Just then my hands found the top of the ladder and I whispered for Leanna to run! I jumped off the ladder without touching the last three steps. We ran and ran all the way home. Never again would I place my hand in another birds nest. Leanna was sworn to secrecy. We would never tell Mama about this moment.

In the evening, when the sun had decided to set, Leanna and I sat on the wrap around porch and kept watch. Finally, there she was. A small, dark shadow walking slowly appeared in the horizon. I didn't realize at the time how tired she must have been. I'd jump up with glee and run with all my might! Leanna would trail behind. There in the distance came my Mama and as always, carrying a small bag of hard candy. As I hugged Mama, she had that Mama smell. How can you describe that? That wonderful smell that belongs only to one's Mother. No one smelled as wonderful as she! With arms around Mama, we slowly walked home with night approaching.

At night after the dishes were put away and the chores were finished, Mama gathered us together. She sat on the weathered oak porch swing as we'd wait with anticipation. This was my favorite time. Time to sit and hug Mama's legs as Leanna and I were perched on the cool floor at Mama's feet. Some of the older girls sat at Mama's side while the rest leaned against the wall. The night crickets sang softly with the echoes of conversation. Mama read the Bible as the oil lamps flicker. Like chicks around a mother hen and spiritual food she gave, what a peaceful feeling this was....

Chapter Three

A few years had gone by and the depression was in full swing. Off in the distance you'd see the smoke billow high into the air from the train that came through a couple of times each day. Hobos made a habit of hopping off the train and walking over to our house. They knew that Mama would, at least, have some corn bread for them to stick in their ragged pockets and a cool drink of water. After sitting a spell on the porch, they thanked Mama and went down the winding railroad track. I figured that they knew when the next train was coming and they'd just hop on. Mama said "Give and ye shall receive." Mama should receive a lot with all the giving she did.

Planting season had arrived in our small town of Flannery. Even with all of us youngins to work the farm, it still was never enough. We needed extra hands for all the garden work. The neighborhood boys were more than eager to help. They would beg their Mamas to let them work our farm. Up the road they came, grinning from ear to ear. They would argue amongst themselves about who was going to stand beside which sister while planting. Each girl was pretty and looked so much alike, I couldn't understand why it mattered which girl they stood beside!

The rows in our garden seemed to stretch into the horizon. What a hot, tedious job this planting was! Mama gave Leanna and me a small corner of the garden to plant our seeds. We planted radishes and lettuce. We'd drop the small seed and cover each one carefully with the soft, black dirt. We felt proud when we'd gotten through. Mama would prepare fresh lemonade when the daily work was done. The cold, sweet taste sure went down easy and could without a doubt cool off a sweaty face.

Our tobacco crop was another story. Since the depression was raging, a lot of local men were out of jobs. Mama hired a few of them to do the winter burning over the land to prepare for our next crop. They plowed and replowed to turn soil while adding fertilizer.

Now that spring had arrived they planted seeds and covered them with cloth until sprouting. There are always big problems with worms and the men picked them off in buckets, green ugly things. They discovered that the best way of getting rid of those worms was with the turkeys and the guineas. They just let them loose in the tobacco garden and they'd get fat eating all those big green worms.

When each day was finished, it's common practice to have the workers stay for dinner. They were so thankful for the work and the southern cooking. It almost seemed as if they were family because we saw them so much. They would continue to work with us through our harvest season.

Harvest time was always a very exciting time on our farm. Men would be out early in the morning as the sun rose in the sky and would still be working after the sun set, cutting these large, leafy tobacco stalks. They would take them and string them upside down in the curing barn to dry.

After the tobacco dried, it was then taken to the market to sell. Mama was a shrewd business woman. She dressed up in her finest dress with every hair brushed neatly and swept up with a comb. A matching hat always graced her head.

Upon arrival at the market, the bidding would begin. Mama would always have a debate before accepting a bid on her burley tobacco. Sometimes you'd see the men's faces turn somewhat red as they breathed heavily. They thought they could pull one over on this tiny dark haired woman with no husband at her side. How wrong they were! They made offers and counter offers to Mama. She considered each offer until she found one that was fair. Mama always got paid what she knew the crop was worth and settled for nothing less.

The men who had so diligently worked the tobacco farm awaited Mama's arrival. She thanked each one as she paid them their due wages. This was always a happy time for everyone. Afterward, we'd all sit around as Mama would get out the Sears catalog because it was time for new shoes and cloth for dresses. We were so blessed.

Saturday evenings were warm and breezy in the summer. After all the chores were complete, the older sisters would clean up, and put on a touch of rouge and lipstick. Dresses were pressed and looked so beautiful on each slender body with hair adorned neatly with combs in place. The Victrola record player would be carried onto the big wrap around porch. Leanna and I just wore our shorts and blouses. We really didn't care about how we looked.

Just like clockwork, up the dirt road that ran in front of our home came the neighborhood boys. They walked leisurely and started up small talk. These were the same young boys that helped with our garden. They, too, looked all neat with shirts tucked into their pants. A hint of hair oil gleamed on each head. They all looked like they were going to church to me. Leanna and I would poke fun as the boys would come onto the porch and stand shyly by as the records began to play. Slowly, the guys and girls paired off and began small talk. Before the evening was done, our gray wooden porch came alive! Benny Goodman's clarinet was heard all over our farm as the song "Sing, Sing, Sing," radiated from the record player followed by the brass section with its loud and boisterous sound! The music literally echoed off the trees. Our little world was vibrant and alive. The boys and girls danced, skirts whirled around. They only stopped for an occasional drink of punch then danced throughout the evening. Leanna and I thought they were funny. We randomly pulled their skirts or poked their backs. Then, we ran fast down the stairs and out into the shelter of the lush, green grass.

Sometimes we hid behind the flower boxes Mama had planted. To think they would have even given us a second glance. No, they were having too much fun to even notice we were there. Yes, we surely poked fun, but very soon, life would move on and it would be our turn to dance...

Chapter Four

It was 1944 and Virginia Sams was the best friend I had in the world. Her copper colored, wavy hair gently flowed about her slender shoulders. A heavy dusting of freckles covered her soft, fair skin. She was taller than me and slender. I am only 5'4" so it wasn't too hard to be taller than me.

"Oh Virginia, let's not go to school today, let's take our lunch money and go get a chocolate sundae," I said. She agreed with a sly smile. We were juniors now after skipping two grades in school. School work came easy for us so why not miss a day now and then? We ran down the railroad tracks that lead into our town of Flannery. Just ahead was our town's drugstore. After hiding our books in the soft green grass, I turned the knob to the store and ran inside. Virginia jumped onto one of the stools at the counter and so did I.

The cool, chocolate sundae looked beautiful. It was served in a pressed glass bowl with whipped cream and a cherry gracing the top. How cold and refreshing it tasted after the long walk! I would spoon another cool mouthful as I twirled around on the swivel stools.

"Shouldn't you girls be at school today?" Fred the druggist asked. He was a small man, maybe sixty-ish, with balding gray hair and mustache to match. He had been there as long as I could remember. "Oh, Virginia had this doctors appointment today and Mama said I could go with her," I lied. He just smiled and let it go.

Looking out the window, you could see the train tracks across the road. Camp cars were rolling in! Virginia and I ate fast because we knew that with camp cars came young men. The train took these guys from town to town to work on the train tracks and pick up coal. The train then leaves and hauls the coal to its next destination. The men would live in the camp cars while working in our town.

We hurried and ran outside gathering our books from the grass, careful to straighten our skirts, reapply our lipstick and check each other over for approval. I had on my button down rose flowered dress. It had a rounded collar folded down that revealed my pearl necklace Mama had given me for Christmas. My eyes are clear and green with a small burst of brown surrounding my pupils. My dark hair pulled slightly back on the left side with a comb and my rosy lipstick matched my dress. Belt tightly around my waist, socks folded neatly down and oxfords on, I was ready to see who might be in those camp cars.

We talked and laughed a lot as we made our way down the long road that ran parallel with the railroad tracks. After about a half mile, we noticed the camp cars had come to a halt. We giggled with excitement, and then quickly composed ourselves. We walked very slowly in anticipation as two guys came out and stood on the red caboose of the train. They grinned at us.

"Hi," they said as we slowly approached the train. "Hi yourself," we said. They jumped from the caboose and sauntered leisurely to the road where we were standing. One guy had sandy hair and sea blue eyes with dark brown eyelashes that seemed to float softly upon his cheeks. His mouth looked soft and his teeth perfectly white and straight. He looked to be about 6 ft tall, medium build and had coveralls on. The other guy had dark hair and brown eyes. He was not as tall as the sandy haired man. He had a radiant smile complete with dimples. He also had coveralls on with his work hat cocked slightly to one side. Yeah, he was cute, but the sandy haired man was making my heart race out of control! I wondered if everyone could hear it. I tried to be calm outside while every fiber of my being was suddenly alive and aware. The dark haired guy said his name was Joe. Virginia thought he was a fine specimen of a man. With all the steadiness I could muster, I looked into those blue eyes of the man with sandy hair, I said, "My name is Aura Leigh." 'What a beautiful name for a beautiful girl," he said. "My name is Ben," he replied as he peered into my very soul. His smile slowly began to broaden, as he showed those wonderful, white teeth. I felt off guard, my every movement was being watched. It made me feel uncomfortable yet excited. While Joe and Virginia talked, Ben kind of walked around me as he smiled. "Do you live close by?" "Well, yes I do, just around the bend in the road in the big, white house." "Well, I believe I'll be seeing you soon Miss Aura Leigh," he replied. "I look forward to it," I said softly, scarcely able to get the words out of my mouth.

Virginia smiled and grabbed my arm. "Let's go," she said. It was hard to move my eyes away from his. Never had I had such a feeling! I liked it. I liked it a lot. With that we left and walked quickly away, all the while Virginia's hand pulled on my arm. After we were out of ear shot, we began to talk about what had just happened. Yes, it certainly was worth skipping school for.

Chapter Five

It's Saturday night, chores are done and Virginia was having a birthday party at her house. I couldn't wait! I so loved parties and people. Kurt was my boyfriend and due to pick me up at any moment. As I answered the knock on the door, he looked so handsome. His blue shirt was unbuttoned at the top exposing a very small amount of dark hair on his chest. His hair was as black as night. Yes, he was a fine looking man, I'm thinking as he asks if I'm ready. I had been seeing him since I was thirteen and he was fifteen. Mama made us sit in the parlor with Leanna looking on. She had relaxed in the last few months and let us be by ourselves-like tonight.

Kurt and I had met in the cafeteria at school. He sat with a bunch of guys at a table that was alongside ours which was full of girls as they talked and laughed. Kurt kept looking my way. Virginia nudged me and laughed. Caught up in the whole experience, I said, "What are you looking at?" He got right up and came to our table. I could feel my cheeks as they turned red. He smiled and said, "I'm looking at you, little bit." I was impressed with his confidence and his fine looks. We were an instant item and have been seeing each other ever since.

I've been known as Kurt's girl for quite a long time and I liked him. He was so easy to be with. Kind and considerate, that's Kurt. We were like a pair of comfortable shoes, that's how I felt when I was with him, we just fit.

As we approached Virginia's house we were all smiles. The large, white, two-story home was alive and loud with excitement! We quickly ran up the many steps that lead to her front porch. Through the black screen door, I saw the house was full of people. The record player was playing big band music, people were talking, some dancing.

The house was immaculate. There in the corner stood a dark wooden table with a large chocolate cake placed neatly beside a glass bowl of fruit punch. Doilies graced all the furniture, starched and pressed perfectly. There were lamps with glass crystals hanging as fringe along the bottom. Light flickered upon them making them appear as diamonds in bright sunlight.

Virginia was sixteen and soon I would be also. Why, we were women and we looked it! Just looking about the room I noticed most of the girls had large bosoms and small waists. That was just the way it was around there. It's like it's in the water or something.

A song ended and another began. It was my favorite song, "In the Mood." Kurt lead me easily into the middle of the floor. I looked at him and he grinned with that sideways grin that melted my heart. What a great dancer he was! He said, "Look out, everyone, here we come!" He twirled me all over the floor and people just backed to the side to watch. My skirt whirled with as much excitement as I felt inside. We danced well together, he and I. He could anticipate my every move and I his. As the song ended, I reached up to pull a strand of hair from my face and suddenly, I could feel someone watching me. I look up and there he was.

Kurt left me to go get a smoke and talk with some of his friends. The music seemed to have become softer. The beating of my heart was once again ringing in my ears as I walked over to the man I met at the train. I looked into his intense blue eyes. He looked even better than I remembered. He looked at me as if he could see into my very soul. I felt a little embarrassed and somewhat clumsy. My knees were weak so I looked away. I stood still to gain composure.

He reached his hand out ever so gently and touched my arm. "Hi again," he said. "Hi yourself," I repeated his word quietly, hoping there was no quiver in my voice." "I told you I would be seeing you soon," he stated. "Would you like a lift home Miss Aura Leigh," he asked? "Well yes," I replied without thinking. I would love it. I excused myself briefly before Kurt could come back.

I grabbed Virginia's arm and pulled her to the next room. "Virginia," I said, "Ben wants to drive me home." "Does he have a car," asked Virginia?

"Well he must cause he asked me if I wanted a lift home," I replied.

Riding in cars were few and far between in Flanary. People really thought you were something if you had a car. I knew this Ben was something. He was more than something. He seemed larger than life. My heart skipped a beat every time I looked in his eyes and now I was going to be in the car with this man!

While Virginia whispered to all the girls about me riding in a car with Ben, he and I slipped out the screen door. We walked quickly down the steps. Something had changed and in that moment I had forgotten there was a Kurt. I was in a daze.

"Where is your car?" I asked. He smiled and took my hand. How strong and warm his hand was as it held mine. It felt so secure, like it could protect me and I would be just fine. I looked; however, I could not see a car. He suddenly stopped and he said, "Here we are. Go ahead and climb on." Well it wasn't a car, but a bicycle. I climbed on the handlebars and he peddled me home. With his arms beside me, I knew that no car ride could have ever been so wonderful. The wind blew through my hair. The night air was cool, peaceful, and dark.

We eventually reached my front porch. I hopped off the bike as he followed me to the steps. Even in the darkness I could make out the shape of his handsome face. It was so close to mine as his eyes looked into mine.

"Thank you," I said softly. Ben paused for a moment and leaned so close I could feel his breath on my face. I swallowed hard. "See you Friday at seven," he said. I quietly managed to get "ok" out of my mouth. He bent his head closer. With a slow, deliberate move, he placed his hands on my shoulders and, ever so softly, kissed my cheek. He then withdrew his hands from my shoulders and said "goodnight." Away he peddled off into the darkness. Within a few moments, he was gone. I embraced myself as I stood reflecting the moment, still a bit overwhelmed with the newness of it all.

As I walked up the steps to the porch, I heard the telephone as it rang from inside the house. I quickly opened the screen door and turned the knob on our front door. I ran inside to the telephone. A black telephone sat on white, starched doilies that graced the table by the couch. "Hello?" I answered breathlessly. It was Virginia. "Kurt was really upset when he found out you left with Ben. No--upset would be an understatement… Mad as hell would be more like it," said Virginia in a high pitched voice. "Aura Leigh, what are you going to do?" I really hadn't had time to think about anything. "Gosh Virginia, I don't know," I said quietly, wrapping the telephone cord around my finger. I felt like I was floating on a cloud as I reflected back on Ben's kiss upon my cheek. "What was this Ben like? Did you have a good time," came Virginia's barrage of questions. Just then there was laughter on the other end of the phone. That's the trouble with party lines. You never know whose listening in. "Some busy-body who evidently didn't have a life of their own was listening in," I continued "Let's talk about this tomorrow after I have time to think." With that I hung up and ran swiftly upstairs to my room.

I really didn't know what to do about Kurt. It seemed as if I had been his girl forever. I cared for him very much. He was so kind to me and we had so much fun together.

On the other hand, if I cared so much for Kurt, how could I have just forgotten him and left with Ben? I had never done anything like that before. I didn't understand what had just happened or why. How could I have done such a thing to Kurt? How could I feel so warm and happy and at the same time realize that I had hurt such a good guy. This was new territory and I had no history of being in such a place. What could I do? What kind of girl was I? Yet, all the while I felt so wonderful!

With my mind in a whirl, I undressed and put on my pink cotton nightgown. I began combing my hair in front of the mirror as I sat and reflected upon the day's events. Dancing with Kurt surely felt easy and secure, yet seeing Ben as he stood there, so calm, so confident, just took my breath away! It seemed as if every fiber of my being felt electrically charged, as if I were alive for the very first time, or, at least, in a way that I had never known. What was this feeling? Oh, what was I doing? What a night!

I turned off the lamp, walked over and threw myself between the clean crisp sheets of my feather bed. I pulled the patchwork quilt Mama had made up to my neck, tucking it securely under my chin. A gentle breeze blew softly through my bedroom window as I eventually drifted off to sleep.

Chapter Six

"Are you going to sleep all day?" Leanna said as she shook my right shoulder vigorously. I rolled over slowly looking at my beautiful thirteen year old sister with her dark hair cascading about her slender shoulders. She had a perfect little turned up nose and smooth, even complexion. My, she was a beautiful girl and she's not even aware of it. In a way, I think this makes her even more attractive. I smiled as I reached up giving her a big hug. "What's that for," she asked inquisitively? "It's because I love you so." "Oh," she said hesitantly, looking perplexed. As sisters go, we take love for granted and sometimes these things just don't come to mind to say.

Growing up, I was closer to Leanna than the rest of my sisters, probably due to our closeness of age. From my very first thoughts she was there. We played and had so much fun on the farm. I always could run faster, jump higher, simply because I was older than her. If I had trouble sleeping at night, it was my sister Leanna that would whisper with me in the shadows. We'd huddle close on cold winter nights as the fireplace would flicker about the room sending hope of warmth to find our bed. How quickly time has gotten away from us. Back to reality.

"I love you too," Leanna stated, "Kurt's on the phone and says he has to talk to you right now."

"Ok I will…well…just tell Kurt I'll call him back," I say quietly.

"He's not going to like it Aura Leigh," replied Leanna.

The bedroom door shut quickly as she ran out of the room. Her footsteps became quieter with each step as she continued down the stairs to the phone…the phone… No, I cannot bring myself to talk to Kurt. Not now. I knew he was hurt and soon I would be more sympathetic to his feelings. This was selfish, I know. I just liked my today's reality. The feeling of newness of life and happy thoughts were dancing in my head. I didn't want anything to take that feeling away. Not now. I stretched slowly, and began to pull the patchwork quilt back from my legs.

What a wonderful quilt with soft pastel patterns. This was made from leftover material Mama used for our family's clothes. How happy we were with each dress that came from her labor, as she sewed on that big black sewing machine! Her small foot would rhythmically rock back and forth weaving thread into each fabric. What a soothing rhythm was there. The love and perfection Mama sewed in each stitch. I could look at each square and there'd be a memory.

I paused as I got up and hugged myself, as I remembered the wonderful night before. I touched my cheek and again, hugged myself. I thought of what a wonderful life I had. While getting dressed, I felt as if I were floating on a cloud and at that moment, saw no chance of coming down.

I held onto the banister as I ran down the stairs, I saw everyone busy with Saturday chores.

"Well," Gail said. "Get a dust cloth and get to work! I thought you were going to sleep all day, Aura Leigh."

I could smell Mama's cooking coming from the kitchen. Nobody's cooking could smell as good as Mama's. Impulsively, I ran into the kitchen and threw my arms about her neck! She was fifty-four now and still strikingly attractive. Her peppered hair was pinned up neatly in the back, and she had a white apron over top of her aqua colored dress. Even with all the cooking Mama had done, the kitchen still sparkled!

Mama stepped back and took a long look at me. "Something is different about you today Aura Leigh, she said."

"Oh Mama, last night I met the most wonderful guy at Virginia's party," I began. "His name is Ben and he has sandy hair and the prettiest eyes I have ever looked into. He wants to see me Friday night," I said as my voice gets a little quieter. I want you to meet him Mama. I know you will like him just as I do."

She put her soft hands around me and held me close. "I'd be happy to meet this boy," Mama said. She continued, "But I thought you and Kurt liked each other." She held me at arms length. As her arms dropped to her sides, I walked over and sat in a chair at the table as I faced her. "I like Kurt, Mama…well, I did. I just am so confused."

Mama laughed, "You're young Aura Leigh. You may have many more boyfriends before you settle for one. That is what I want you to do. These are the happiest days of your life, Aura Leigh. Enjoy them while they are here. Time has a way of marching on and soon these days will all be just a memory."

We talked a little more, and then I got up, walked over to her as she stood in front of the stove. I wrapped my arms around my sweet little Mama. How wonderful she smelled. I hoped that I smelled half as good as she. While enjoying the hug, I reached behind her taking hold of a warm buttermilk biscuit that sat on the stove. I excused myself and ran from the kitchen with the biscuit hidden discreetly in my hand. How warm and wonderful it tasted. How happy I was that day!

Chapter Seven

It was a warm spring Monday morning as Virginia and I walked down the old dirt road leading to our school. The young green leaves hung securely on the trees as the sun filtered through them and created shadows around us. We talked about the party, and about Ben. I told her how secure I felt with his arms about me as he peddled me home on his bike. I told Virginia how soft Ben's lips were when they graced my cheek. We both giggled. Virginia said she wanted to see Ben's coworker Joe again. I said that could be arranged.

"We'll just go walking down by the camp cars after school and maybe they will see us," I said. We walked leisurely on to school.

As we approached the school, I began to get apprehensive. I had eluded Kurt's calls all weekend and I knew today was the day I would see him. No way around it. He was a senior and I a junior. In a small school like ours, you saw everybody that's in it. Sure enough as Virginia and I neared the building, Kurt was leaning against the side of the school wall.

"Hey Aura Leigh," Kurt shouted.

"Hey Kurt," I said meekly as we approached him cautiously. His mouth was drawn in a straight line, with a cigarette hanging from the corner of his mouth. He took a big draw from his cigarette then threw it on the ground and crushed it with his foot. The smoke blew furiously from his mouth as his eyes met mine and, without words, said everything. I did not know what to say and I sure wasn't going to start off the conversation. However, Kurt was more than ready to talk.

"Where the hell have you been all weekend and why ain't you returned any of my calls?" Kurt yelled. "You just left me standing in the corner with my friends and snuck out of the party with some guy! You didn't say goodbye, kiss my ass or nothing! Are you crazy, Aura Leigh? What about us? Don't I mean anything to you? I thought it was you and me. We have never even had one problem in our relationship and you just left me looking like a fool and go off with a total stranger! I ain't going to stand for this Aura Leigh. I just ain't."

After Kurt had finished yelling, he just stood there with shoulders slumped, like the air just went out of him. "We'll talk soon," I stammered.

"No Aura Leigh, we will talk this evening, a nice LONG talk. We'll meet right here after school," he said in a matter of fact tone.

"Yes Kurt" was all I managed to get out just as the bell rang. Saved by the bell, I thought.

Once in the building, Virginia looped her arm into mine and pulled me up the hall. "What on earth are you going to do, she whispered?"

"I don't know, Virginia" I stated. I have liked Kurt as long as I can remember. I still do. "Oh Virginia, It's so confusing! But this thing with Ben feels totally different. There was so much joy and excitement at the very thought of him." At that Virginia and I walked into class and took our seats side by side.

School was interesting to me. It looked like I would be graduating just before my seventeenth birthday. That was great for me. Even though I enjoyed it, I had always looked forward to finishing school and getting married.

Home-Economics was my favorite course. We cut pictures from a catalog and pasted them into a scrapbook. It showed what we wanted our future home to look like. So far, I had made my kitchen, living room, and now I am working on my bathroom. Wow! Wouldn't that be special? To have a toilet inside with running water and to have a tub that you could just get in without having to carry it from the back porch.

We have always had a toilet. It's a nice outdoor toilet made out of wood. The lock was a small, rectangular piece of wood on the door with a nail in the center to secure it. You just turn the lock to keep people out. Our toilet is a two seater. Virginia and I sometimes went to the toilet together. There's a lot of talking you can do sitting side by side on a two seater toilet. We've solved many a problem through the years in that outhouse.

Now, back to my scrapbook. I have cut out a beautiful clawfoot bathtub for my house with an inside toilet as well. It made me happy just planning this house, knowing it may not be too far away in my future. Gosh, wonder who I will share this house with? This wonderful house I have put together inside this notebook. Kurt or Ben? Ben or Kurt? Kurt was so easy with his warm and knowing smile and thick dark hair, always neatly combed with the glint of hair oil. I could just step in his stride and I felt like I was home.

Ben, on the other hand, well, he seemed like an adventure. He appeared a little reckless and yet so sure of himself. I felt excited yet unsettled when I was around him. Wonder what kind of life that would be married to a guy like him. So much I had to think about.

The bell rang and the end of the school day was here. I slowly got to my feet and I turned to Virginia. "Go, with me," I said.

"Okay" Virginia replied quietly.

As we start walking out of the building, I saw Kurt making great strides toward us. "You'll have to walk yourself home today Virginia," Kurt said.

"Hi," I said quietly.

"So what's it going to be Aura Leigh?" He said while taking hold of my arm.

"Kurt, I have thought about this all day and I need to be totally honest with you. I have always cared for you. You are an easy and comfortable guy to be with."

"I don't want you to think of me as comfortable Aura Leigh," Kurt stated strongly.

"Kurt, I feel more than that for you and you know it. I care deeply for you. You are all I have ever known in a boyfriend and I have enjoyed our lives together as a couple. Truly I have. It's just that I have met this guy and I need to tell you, I have never felt like this before. I am sorry Kurt, but I have to figure out what this is that I am feeling. If I don't, I'll always wonder. It would be there in the back of my mind and in my heart. I just have to know, Kurt. It would not be fair to you or me otherwise. I didn't mean for this to happen Kurt. I am truly sorry."

"You are my girl Aura Leigh!" Kurt shouted. "How can I just sit by while you start seeing this railroad hoodlum? He ain't even in school."

"He's not a hoodlum Kurt," I said. "He may have already finished school—I don't know."

Kurt's eyes widened as his voice grew even louder, "You don't even know much of anything about this –whatever he is and you are ready to just throw us away? Aura Leigh, I think you've gone crazy. Well I for one am not going to stand on the sidelines and wait while you're seeing this asshole," He continued. "There are many fish in the sea and I will have no trouble reeling whoever I want in. You'll regret this Aura Leigh. Mark my words this day---You will regret this!"

In some, perhaps small, way I knew what Kurt had said was true. The girls at school always talked about how lucky I was to have Kurt. He was so handsome, good physique, and was a good person. He is such a great dancer and a crowd pleaser. Good looking and always fun. That's my Kurt. I never thought of him with another girl. Could I handle that? What am I doing? I felt this was dangerous territory I was crossing. Just then Kurt breaks into my thoughts.

"When you decide it's me you want to be with Aura Leigh, it just may be too late," He stated and with that, he turned and walked away. I watched him as he walked down the road. His aggressive stride showed he was mad as hell. Never had I seen him upset like that. I hated doing this to Kurt-to us. Why did life throw such curves at you? I was sure I couldn't figure it out. At that, Virginia came walked up quickly from a side road where she'd been anxiously waiting.

"What happened? She asked. "I don't know Virginia. "Maybe I'm just messing up my whole life," I said as I went on. "I just feel like I don't have a choice." We walked in silence lost in thought down the winding dirt road.

That evening I spent most of my time alone and in deep thought. I felt just awful and I had never hurt anyone like this before. I knew others that had broken up before but never realized just how terrible it could make you feel. My thoughts were consumed with Kurt and Ben and the decision that I had made. Eventually, I settled into bed and thought of something I had often heard Mama say when life has become difficult. I whisper aloud "this too shall pass."

In a short time my mind calmed and sleep found me.

The next day, thoughts of Ben kept me from paying attention in class. When school let out, I was grateful to have not seen Kurt. Like always, I walked with Virginia. On the way home, our road became parallel to the train tracks. We walked by the camp cars and saw Ben and Joe as they sat on the steps of the train. They were both eating bologna sandwiches and drinking coffee.

"Hi," Ben said.

"Hi yourself," I said smiling. Ben had on blue coveralls and was clearly dirty from working all day. But still, he was so handsome. Just looking at him, I felt excitement from head to toe. I instinctively touched my cheek and remembered the moment his lips softly rested there.

"Friday night will be here before we know it, Aura Leigh," Ben said with a broad smile crossing his face.

Virginia and I stood closely looking down at the guys as they sat leisurely on the train steps. "Yea, I know," I said as a warm glow rose slowly to my cheeks. Both guys stood up and sauntered forward until they were very close, however it was a comfortable closeness.

"Virginia," Joe began, "What do you say you meet me at Aura Leigh's Friday too and we'll all do something together."

"Joe—I'd like that," Virginia said quietly with a soft smile and her green eyes sparkled.

"Then we'll see you ladies Friday evening at seven," Ben stated as he looked into my eyes. His right hand rested easily on my left shoulder. He gave it a soft squeeze. God, the electricity in that hand! As his hand relaxed, we said our goodbyes and were on our way.

Virginia talked a mile a minute. "Talk quietly and act normal, Virginia," I continued. "You know they are watching our every step! Let's walk slow and deliberate, like we don't have a care in the world," I giggled softly. We smiled and used our most confident stride as we walked away.

Chapter Eight

My goodness, it's Friday I thought as I lay in bed looking up at the ceiling. All around were butterfly prints from my sheer curtains which the wind softly blew them around by my window. The sun had filtered through and caused the happy prints to dance about the room. It's as if God knew what today would mean to me and he was casting a broad luminous smile over the earth. Did I get any sleep last night I wondered as I lay on my right side, elbow on the bed and my head resting on my head as I looked out the window? The hours had seemed to crawl as my mind would race and in deep thought – I planned in my head what this day would bring. I should have felt exhausted, but no. Invigorated, energized, happy –those were just some of the feelings that came to mind. I got to get up and get ready for school. There's just something about thinking and planning. Where would Ben and I go? What would I feel when he comes to the door? I prayed I would look confident, even though inside I would be jelly. Very soon I'd feel his touch? Thinking about Ben was almost as exciting as being with him, well almost.

School went by pretty much uneventful- that is, until it was over. Virginia and I were leaving the building, happily holding onto one another with unending conversation when we both felt someone peering at us. I looked and there he was. Kurt with a couple guys talking and looking our way. His face had a seriously mad look about it. "You girls seem to be mighty happy today," he shouted.

"Well it is Friday, Kurt, we're happy schools out for the weekend." I stammered.

"Hell yeah, that's why we all are so damn happy," he shouted. I just looked at him and felt numb. To think I was his girl just days ago. We seem miles apart now. Virginia breaks into my thoughts, "Aura Leigh, let's stop by my place and get my clothes. I'll just go to your house and get ready with you," she giggled.

As I ran up all those steps that led to her house, it all came back to me. That wonderful night of the party. Ben's hand was holding tightly to mine, while running down these wonderful stairs. It made me want to stop and kiss each step. I now loved each one because I knew Ben's foot had been on them.

I plopped on Virginia's bed as she threw open the closet. Aura Leigh, she began, "What should I wear?" she stated as she took dresses, skirts, blouses one by one out of the closet and held them next to her. She stood in front of a large round mirror attached to dark mahogany dresser. I knew for sure, this would take a while.

Putting on my last bit of rouge by my round dresser mirror, I looked out of the corner of my eye and saw Virginia looking at me. "Wow Aura Leigh, you look so pretty," said Virginia with a broad smile graced that wonderful freckled face. And she did too. Standing in my light, airy bedroom I thought Virginia reminded me of a porcelain doll. Virginia had decided to wear a dark emerald green dress with a matching belt. Her hair was in a pageboy that parted on the side and neatly folded under. It had such a deep lovely red color! Those large green eyes of hers danced which mirrored the color of her dress. Yes, I did feel attractive I thought as I tucked my black and white blouse into my solid black skirt. My blouse was tapered which accentuated my large bust and small waist, complete with thin, black belt. We checked the seams in back of our hose, garters intact, heels on, we were looking good! My small black hat was tilted to the side as my dark curls softly gathered about my face.

"It's six forty-five! Oh my God Virginia, I think I might just faint. I feel flushed, my face feels hot and I must look awful nervous!" I blurted out as I paced the living room floor.

"Oh, you look calm on the outside and your face isn't flushed at all," Virginia replied calmly in a reassuring way. We continued to walk apprehensively about the room, straightening our skirts and all the while we halfway smiled. As I glanced at Virginia from the corner of my eye, she looked as nervous as I felt. I didn't let on that she looked anything but confident. I peeked unassumingly out the side of the curtain by the window. All was dark outside and I couldn't see a thing. I moved away from the window and just leaned against the wall.

Sure enough, the time was seven o'clock. There were three deliberate knocks on the door. I took hold of Virginia's arm. "Don't answer too quickly," I whispered. "We don't want to look like we are perched at the door." I began to count. One-one thousand, two-one thousand three-one thousand, until five, then I took in a deep breath and slowly exhaled. I was decidedly relaxed for appearance sake and opened the door.

Ben was in front with Joe right behind. "Hi fellows," I said grinning. "Please come in. I looked up at Ben while holding the door open. He walked by me – looking into my eyes. His eyes were full of excitement! It was as if they knew a secret and would not let me in on it. My heart just leaped. Joe sauntered in and gave Virginia the once over. "My, my, my," Joe went on, "Ain't you a pretty little thing." Virginia's face became as red as her hair. We all laughed just as Mama came in from the kitchen.

"Good evening boys," Mama said. How are you this evening?

Ben walked over and extended his hand to my mother. "My name is Ben, ma'am, and I am fine."

"Well I have heard nice things about you Ben," Mama said with her confident smile. "Would you all like something to drink?" Mama asked.

"No ma'am, we want to catch a movie in Flannery and have a cab waiting, but we'll take a rain check," replied Ben.

"I'll hold you to it," said my Mama. I gave her a big hug, and promised in her ear, I would not be late. I told her I loved her and she gave me a knowing smile. She liked Ben already. I was sure of it.

Virginia and I looked at each other with great anticipation! We did not know we were going to the movies. It just seemed a perfect thing to do. Ben held the door as I walked out.

Joe and Virginia followed, but quickly passed me up. They ran down the stairs, off the porch and into the cab. Ben walked up from behind me and placed his arm about my shoulders as my hand seemed to glide naturally to his waist. We walked off the porch and down the steps and into the cab.

We all four sat in the back of the taxi. It was a little bit of a squeeze, but no one minded and no one wanted to sit in the front. Joe and Virginia were already engaged in conversation as I looked up at Ben's face. His arm was about my shoulder and my head rested on his chest. "How was your day, Ben?" I asked.

"Joe and I had a busy day," he began. "We were doing track sections, driving spikes and cutting brush. It went quickly with all the talk we did about you girls. All week the guys in the camp cars have been ribbing us about you both. They saw you all the other day when you walked by the train and talked to us. That night when we were all sitting around playing cards, well, that was when it was the worst. George and Larry kept telling us what good looking women you were and how they were going to move in on our territory." We just laughed and said, "You guys are just jealous, couldn't buy yourselves a woman, much less take ours."

We love working in Flannery, Aura Leigh. We hook up to one of the houses by the tracks and have electricity which is a rare thing. Sure is nice to be able to have light and the stove working in the camp cars. George is our cook. He says the cooking sure was easier when you can do it inside, especially if there comes a rain. Potatoes just ain't as good with water in them. Ben lit up that amazing smile. "Also, he continued, at night after work is done, us guys sit around playing cards. Well, let's just say, the guys would think twice about cheating when there's a good strong light. I'd say that's why some would rather play cards with the lamp. Not me. Give me a good light. I am a very good player, maybe even the best. I don't have to cheat to win Aura Leigh. Winning just comes natural for me when it comes to poker," Ben smiled again. I settled in the bend of Ben's arm as he continued to talk.

"You all have that cool creek here in Flannery complete with a waterfall by the mountainside. We guys look forward to going there after a hard day's work. We just jump in with our octagon soap and lather up up in the cool water and swim about to rinse off."

"You mean to tell me that you guys bathe in our creek without clothes on?" I said with a surprised grin on my face.

Ben squeezed my shoulder and with a wink stated, "You should come join me sometime."

I hit Ben on the shoulder in a shy playful way. We laughed for a minute and then settled back in.

"Yep, there is no better place we would rather park the train than Flannery. The women aren't too bad either," Ben said as he looked me up and down. I felt warmth flood my body while he drank me in. I was crazy about this man and I knew it. I eased my head down and rested it once again on his broad, strong shoulder.

How clean this man smelled. Was it because he just talked about bathing? No, he just was. Even when I saw him at work dirty, he still had a clean smell. I loved that, I thought. We eased into a quiet ride as the cab driver drove through the curvy, narrow roads. The moon was yellow, full and large. The shadows of passing trees came and went across the back seat. How romantic this all was. I didn't care if we ever got to the movies. It couldn't get any better than at this moment in time.

Jane Eyre was the movie that played. We all sat in a row with Virginia and me in the middle. We'd grin at each other from time to time. I knew she was enjoying Joe. She looked so alive and vibrant. It was such a touching story –a romantic drama. I could feel Ben's every movement beside me. I was in his space and drawn like a moth to a flame. The movie was compelling. We all did watch intently. Well, with my head permanently fixed to his shoulder and his hand warm about me. He rested his face to the side of my head and from time to time I could feel his warm breath upon my hair and his lips would softly touch my forehead.

We walked briskly, arm in arm after the movie. It was such a clear night and the guys wanted ice cream. Virginia and I excused ourselves after going into the drug store. The guys waited on the swivel stools as we walked into the restroom. "Aura Leigh, Joe is incredible, funny, and handsome and I like him!" Virginia said as she gave me a hug. We smiled at each other.

"I know. God, I so know how you feel," I went on. "Ben is the most attractive man on the planet!"

"Well that's debatable," laughed Virginia. We reapplied lipstick, fixed our hair and gave each other a quick hug. Happy had to take a backseat to the intense joy that we all felt that night. This was a time we'd reflect back on and cherish forever.

We laughed and talked with each other as we ate the ice cream and walked to the cab stand. Joe gave Virginia a bite of his ice-cream and then eased it gently, closer to her face, and ice-cream rested on her nose. After she wiped her nose with a tissue she took off and chased him. He ran with arms flailing—the ice-cream fell right off the cone. She caught him, now thinking back—I am sure he let her. He just put his arms around her and kissed her nose first, and then went right to her mouth.

Ben turned me to face him. His face so close, I could hardly see him. "Aura Leigh," he began, "I am crazy about you" He ever so gently cupped his hands about my face and softly kissed me. His kiss was warm and gentle. His hands pulled me next to him. His kisses became more intense. My head was spinning and I didn't want it to stop. "Oh God" was all I managed to get out. He held me tightly for a moment then very slowly and softly, released me. Then arm in arm we walked the cool quiet street that lead to the cab stand.

They said goodnight at the door. I hated to see them leave….to see him leave. "I'll see you tomorrow Aura Leigh," Ben said matter of fact.

(Thinking fast thinking Mama may not let me see Ben again so soon), I replied, "Well, after chores are done, Virginia and I will take a walk by your camp cars," I said. "I just don't know what time we will get finished."

"Ok," said Ben. "We will look for you girls tomorrow then." Ben and Joe smiled at each other and then at us. Another long wonderful goodnight kiss and off they went into the night.

Virginia and I entered into the house quietly, ascended up the stairs and fell onto my bed. The night was so wonderful that it left us speechless, perhaps for the first time in our lives.

Chapter Nine

Fall became winter – winter became spring and the train took Ben further and further away from Flannery to work. Sometimes he would be gone for weeks, though he always remembered to write. I received a letter almost each and every day. I would kiss and cherish each and every page. I kept all his letters tied up in a red ribbon and placed into a wooden box with red velvet interior. I would watch for old # 6 train to come rolling in. When it arrived, I would run with all my might to get to the train steps. Ben would jump off and swing me around. With hugs, kisses we'd walk off arm in arm. The hours would seem to turn into minutes while we sat on the front porch swing and listened to the crickets and watched the stars. Sometimes, Ben would bring his guitar and sing to me. He had funny songs and sometimes he'd sing love songs. He had a wonderful voice and was a very confident guitar player. His fingers would strum effortlessly across the strings. I so loved that. I would sing with him sometimes and we had quite a nice harmony together. It was a magical feeling. Some evenings we'd walk to the creek and put our feet in. We'd splash each other, laugh and play like two children. What fun we had and then began our share of arguments. The arguments had merit-at least for me.

There was talk that Ben had been seeing a girl from his home town on the weeks when his train didn't make it to Flannery. This thought made me furious! How could he hold another woman if he felt by me like I did him? This made me nauseated to my very soul. After a heated argument where Ben swore, denied, and yelled that there wasn't and couldn't be another woman, he finally looked like the air had left his body. I guess there was no fight left in him. He looked at me and believed that I already knew. Maybe I did know somewhere deep inside. It truly hadn't completely made it to my heart yet, at least not until he quietly admitted it. The admission of his unfaithfulness seemed so unreal!

When I was Kurt's girl, I never had to deal with even the thought of another woman. I just could not imagine Ben doing this to me-to us. He hung his head and softly said it was out of loneliness and it meant absolutely nothing. He said he would not see her again.

"What about me and the loneliness I have felt night after night when you were not here," I shouted, "You son of a bitch!" I took off and ran down the railroad track.

Ben came after me and caught me with his strong grip. "I'm so sorry," he began.

Tears streamed down my face as I slapped him hard! "I hope that hurt like hell. Don't you write me, don't you call me, don't you come see me any more Ben!" I screamed. "This is it!" I left him standing there. I marched off quickly, tears pouring, without end; down my face I cried all the way home.

As time went by, I became increasingly lonely. Kurt found out that Ben and I had broken up. He called me and slowly, I began to see him again. I did this partly to get back at Ben, I imagine, and also because I enjoyed Kurt's company. It was so nice being with Kurt. It was comfortable and I knew that I could trust him. Kurt was even more handsome than I remembered with his dark hair and his crooked smile. He was also a very good kisser. It just seemed to lack that magnetic feeling that was there when Ben had kissed me. That, of course, was a secret that I would never let Kurt know.

When night approached, that was the hardest time for me. I would lie in bed each night, the thoughts of Ben never far from my mind and they haunted me to my core. I literally ached for him. I wondered if he ever thought of me. How could he not? His touch left such a sensation about my body. Didn't he feel that too? Could a person feel that feeling alone? Could I have loved him so much and it not have been returned? I would then get mad at me for even thinking of Ben and I counseled myself. "I should be thinking of Kurt and his goodness, not Ben!" I remained frustrated as the darkness enveloped me.

What a beautiful day it was as Kurt and I lay with our heads on a log that rested against the spring house. We gazed up at the white clouds and imagined what each cloud looked like. "That one looks like a dog," I said.

He laughed, "I think it kind of looks like you Aura Leigh." Kurt replied as he grinned. I pushed him and he began tickling me. We laughed and relaxed as we enjoyed each others company. Kurt looked at me intently. "Aura Leigh I have always loved you," Kurt said softly. "I am and have always been the man for you." He took my hand and kissed it softly and then gave me a long, warm kiss. It felt good to be kissed by Kurt again. He was so handsome and easy to be with. No emotional roller coaster with him. You knew where you stood with this man.

"Kurt, I love you too," I said slowly. "I am just not sure if I am in love with you." I saw his eyes darken and his lips press together in a straight line. After a few moments he said, "I believe you love me, Aura Leigh, and are in love with me. You just don't know it."

"Well, you may be right," I said. "I am so confused about life," I went on as an after-thought. He took my hand and helped me up from the log.

We walked quietly down the road to a large creek. Removing our shoes we set them on the soft grass. The waterfall cascaded briskly into the water's edge and sent droplets that sprayed out over the rocks where Kurt and I walked. It felt refreshing to have the cool water fall in small beads about my face and hair.

"I must look a mess." "No Aura Leigh, You look beautiful."

Chapter Ten

"Virginia, in just a month we will be graduating! Can you believe it?" I said as we are walked to school with books in hand.

"I know Aura Leigh," she goes on. "Are you going to marry Kurt?"

"Gosh, Virginia I just don't know… He has talked about it many times. He is a wonderful man. Well he's just about everything a woman could want and more! Why wouldn't I marry him Virginia?"

"Because you still love Ben," Virginia said slowly."

"God Virginia, do you think I do?"

"Joe said you're all Ben talks about, that since you broke up with him he just mopes about, don't eat much. Why he won't even play poker with the guys," stated Virginia.

"How could I ever trust him again?" I said quietly. "I just can't understand why excitement stirs in my stomach at the very thought of him."

"Oh, it's love," replied Virginia matter of fact. "You care for Kurt and I am sure of that, but it's Ben that's got your heart."

I paused as I thought about what Virginia had just said. I hadn't talked to Ben when he called and not one letter did I answer. Though I didn't let myself read them, the letters had continued to come from Ben. I couldn't seem to throw them away, so I had placed them unopened in my wooden box. I also had avoided the train. Yes, I had been proud of myself with all the avoiding I had been doing. And now Virginia's words, they haunted me. I had even tried to pray Ben out of my heart.

"I am trying so hard to get over Ben--Virginia; and you are my best friend in the world. Please help me get over Ben. Help me do the right thing for myself."

"Honey, the heart is a treacherous thing, it wants what it wants and your heart wants Ben," replied Virginia matter of factly. "There is nothing even a best friend can do about that." We walked the rest of the way in silence. However, my mind was anything but silent.

School went by quickly. Kurt had graduated the year before and was now a coal miner. Of course it worried me that he chose the mines. The dangers were plenty and I knew that firsthand with my brother Henry. The guys would travel miles deep into the mine shaft. I couldn't imagine working all day with the earth over my head. At any moment one of the timbers might break and the rockfall could end his life, just like my brother's. It was a big fear of mine that Kurt never paid any attention to. He'd just laugh and say, "You run the direction the rats run. They seem to know if there is going to be a rockfall before a sound is made. You just see them running and you go too. Those rats will save your life," he'd say.

Kurt wanted me to graduate and was proud of me and told me so often. He then wanted me to marry him and I told him I was thinking about it all. I did think about it---then I'd see Ben's face. I must have been moving slow, for Virginia broke into my thoughts, "Let's get walking, Aura Leigh."

"Alright girl, let's go" I said.

We had almost made it home, taking our dirt road home which ran parallel to the train tracks. The camp cars were on the tracks and I stopped. "I got to turn around. I can't go by that train! What if Ben is in there? I whispered under my breath.

"Don't be silly, Aura Leigh. This is our only way home." replied Virginia.

"Please, let's be quiet just in case." I said cautiously. I knew I did not, could not see Ben. I was safe if he stayed away. I knew this, I thought. Just at that very moment Joe came out of one of the cars with Ben behind him stopping on the top stair.

"Hey, Joe Honey," replies Virginia as she ran up and throws her arms about him. He gave her a wonderful hug and they giggled and began talking. I felt uneasy as I just stood there with my legs getting weaker. A large lump was in my throat as I looked up and saw Ben looking at me. "How are you Aura Leigh?" Ben began. I felt awkward as he walked down the stairs and came closer and closer to me. I didn't move. I didn't dare speak. I was afraid my heart would give me away. I surely never wanted him to know how much I had missed him, how the very thought of him sent me reeling. And now he is here and I cannot get away. I remained with a million thoughts running through my head. Can't I get away? My legs just didn't seem to want to work. My heart was racing and I could feel it pounding in my chest as well as my head. Oh God, he was going to speak.

"Aura Leigh, I've missed you so," he began. He smelled so good as he walked up and stood before me. I could breathe him in. It was intoxicating. Those blue eyes were gazing into mine. They caught hold of my gaze and simply would not let go. "I am so very sorry that I was unfaithful to you," he went on. "There were weeks that went by that I wasn't stationed in Flannery. I didn't see you and I missed you. I knew it was wrong. It was late one night I was out drinking with the boys. I had too much to drink and she was there. I ain't proud of what I did and can't change what happened." He said as he stepped closer. "I was so far away from you….."

I have needs, Aura Leigh, and I don't expect you to take care of them for me until we are married. I was vulnerable and she was willing. She meant nothing, I swear before God. Please take me back, Aura Leigh, and I will be a faithful man. I will work hard and save. We can get married soon. If I could have you – make love to you. Oh Aura Leigh, that would make me the happiest man in the world. All my needs, all my wants would be with you."

As if Ben knew I felt weak with all the emotion that was surging within me, he placed both hands on my shoulders and looked deeply into my eyes. I remained quiet for composure as my eyes filled with tears and ran silently down my face. He gently took his hand and brushed them away as he kissed my face and then captured my mouth soft yet forcefully with his own. Nothing I had ever experienced up to that point could measure

The passion that was now rose within me. He held me close; his hands first were on my waist and then slid downward, holding me firmly against him. "God, Aura Leigh, he breathed in my ear. I need you so."

Finally, I found my voice and loosened as best I could from his grip. "Ben, you hurt me more than you will ever know," I began. "How can I trust you ever? I don't want to hurt like that again. I- I am seeing Kurt now and he is good and he is faithful."

"Kurt's ass, Aura Leigh, he will never make you feel like I do," Ben stated. "You know that it's true. You are in love with me. It's us. You're mine." I shrugged my shoulders, no fight left in me. I was overcome with the feelings within me. I knew whether this was right or whether it was wrong, these words rang true.

"Ben, I will think about it."

"We will be working in Flannery again next week honey, I will see you then," Ben said and once again held me close. He was much softer this time as he tilted my chin up for one last kiss. As he slowly released me, the look of such love in his eyes, I had to smile. Looking for Virginia to save me, she was close at my side. "Let's go home," I managed to get out.

We began to walk with Virginia's hand around my shoulder. I knew she loved me. I also felt like Virginia wanted me to be with Ben. Maybe it was because Ben and Joe were best friends like Virginia and me. It was kind of a complete circle with the four of us together. I just had that gnawing feeling in the pit of my stomach like something wasn't right.

The house bustled with activity as I arrived in from school. I was about to climb the stairs when I caught Mama's eyes as she looked at me from the kitchen doorway. "Aura Leigh, come talk to me," Mama said.

I walked into the kitchen and sat down at the table beside her. "I can tell something is bothering you child. What is it?" As I talked to Mama about my situation and the decision between Kurt and Ben, she had such a look of understanding. She always did. Even as a child, if I scraped a knee or if someone hurt me, she was always there with that same understanding look. I was so glad I had this woman in my life to listen to me and love me no matter what I did. She was always on my side. My defender, my Mama.

After an exhausting discussion, she told me that it was ultimately my decision. She would support my choice. We hugged for the longest. I breathed her in. That Mama smell ………indescribable!

Chapter Eleven

It was Friday evening and Kurt was off from work. Like every Friday these past few weeks, he'd go home to bathe and then he'd come to see me. Believe me; a coal miner can't just skip a bath. I thought it must be one of the dirtiest jobs one could choose to do.

I dreaded his visit. I couldn't imagine what I would say or how I would say it. What the hell was I going to tell him? I really didn't want to hurt this man again. He was waiting for a reply to marriage and here I was thinking of breaking up again. He had no clue. What was I doing, I asked myself? Was this the right choice for me? Did my heart even give me a choice?

I buttoned my dress and fastened my belt. I looked at myself in the mirror. I was a sixteen year old woman. I had to make a decision and stick with it. I knew the decision would change my life. The crossroads were a lonely place to be. On one hand I had this wonderful handsome man Kurt. He was good, honest and kind. He was everything a girl could ever want or desire. He would be good to me, faithful, loving. He would make a good living, be a wonderful father to our children. A good life I would have. He was everything sensible a girl could possibly want. But was that enough?

The other road would take me to Ben. He was certainly sexy, thrilling. He could make my heart leap at the very thought of him. We could have a good life…..couldn't we?? I felt so alive just to be in his presence. God, help me, I thought as I look at this girl in the mirror. Help me Lord.

Kurt was early as usual. I was ready, which was a change for me. Usually, I was the one who ran behind. I met him at the door. "Aura Leigh, you are ready?"

"Yes," I said grinning at this sweet guy. I felt a rush of such warmth in my heart for Kurt.

"Guess you just couldn't wait to see me," Kurt said smiling.

"That's it," I said. I took his arm as we walked outside. The sunset was the most amazing I had ever seen! The western sky was a brilliant, yet soft red, mixed with varied shades of gray. The sun rays pierced through the clouds at random. The sky cast a rose colored glow all about Kurt and me. It was as if God made this sunset just for us! Never had I seen such a sunset. Never would I again. Its beauty caught me off guard, yet made me feel sad, very sad. "Isn't this a beautiful sunset Kurt," I said as we began walking down the old dirt road.

"Not as beautiful as the girl that is on my arm. I love you Aura Leigh," Kurt said easily.

We held hands as we walked and it felt good. I did not respond and after a few minutes we came upon a maple tree. We sat down and leaned our backs against it.

"What is on your mind tonight, Aura Leigh? It feels good to be with you, but I feel you are somewhere else."

"I'm sorry Kurt," I said. The tears began filling my eyes as I tried to not let him see.

"What is it honey?" Kurt said as he looked at me.

"Kurt, I do love you so much. I know I do." With that I put my arms around him ever so tight as the sun began its slow descent.

Kurt's arms tensed up. "I don't think I even want to hear this," Kurt said. "Surely to God, you are not having second thoughts about us again, Aura Leigh! Not now that we are doing so good and thinking of our lives together." Kurt looked at me and I could not return his gaze. "Don't be stupid. You know me. You love me and I you. I am the man for you; always. We'd have such a wonderful life, Aura Leigh," Kurt stated with astonishment.

"Kurt, there's just no easy way to say this," I started. As I spoke, I lowered my head. "I saw Ben this week. I did not mean to. He came out of the train when I was walking home. He came up to me and insisted on talking to me. I did not want to. I paused and took a deep breath. I have feelings for him. I can't get them out of my head, out of my heart. It is not fair to you, Kurt. It's not even fair to me," I whispered.

"Damn it to hell Aura Leigh," Kurt shouted as he jumped to his feet! This man screws another woman when he is supposed to be promised to you. He is an unfaithful son of a bitch and you know it! I would not, could not do that to you. This choice will be the final choice. If it is him, I will go on with my life. I don't want that. Damn it, I want you to be my wife! But I am not going to have a woman that is constantly thinking of someone else. Is that the way it is, Aura Leigh? You will never get him out of your heart?"

"Kurt, I- I am not in control of these emotions" I said as I managed to get to my feet. "The heart goes where it will and I don't seem to be able to control it."

After a few moments of silence, Kurt faced me. He looked at me for what felt to be an eternity. The anger from his face drained away. No loud words were left. Just love. He took me in his arms one last time and slowly reached for my mouth with his and kissed me so tenderly, so sweetly that tears silently ran down my cheeks. He held me closer to his heart than I had ever been. I could feel his heart beat next to mine. It was a very peaceful moment in time and then, he let me go. "Be happy Aura Leigh, Kurt's voice became softer. Be happy." With that he smiled slightly and walked away. Like the sunset, Kurt was gone. I stood by the tree and saw a man that loved me with his entire heart walk out of my life for the last time. What emptiness was there at that moment.

I felt I really had no choice. I felt the crossroads fade away. I was now on one road only. I wondered where this road would take me in life. As I took my first step…

Chapter Twelve

The air was just crackling with electricity as Virginia and I stood at the train station in Flannery. We checked each other over carefully. Our dark lipstick applied just right really complimented the sharp contrast of our white teeth. Not too much rouge. Our hair combs in place. We looked so different yet good together, I thought. Virginia had her intense, dark red hair and pale, freckled skin. She was taller than me and slim. She always looked like she walked right out of a catalog to me. She knew the clothes to wear that accentuated what she had, which was a lot. Me, well I too was blessed. My dark hair was neatly in place. My olive skin and slender body with large breast completed my package. We were grown women now. We checked each other one last time as we had done throughout our life, today; however, had a new feeling about it. We were graduating in a couple of weeks. Our lives would take different paths. There would be no more Virginia and I running up and down the tracks, making sure each of us was flawless. No--- To leave this wonderful relationship behind and move on seemed unreal. Our whole lives until this point were Virginia and I. She knew my every thought and I hers. Could we even separate from each other and be a whole person? Goodness. I didn't know. She was my right arm and without her there would be a loss no other human could fill. I looked at my friend and could tell she was experiencing the same thoughts.

"Oh, Aura Leigh," Virginia said as she wrapped her arms around me. We held each other tightly as the tears started to flow. Quickly we released each other and opened our purses for tissue. As much as we loved each other, we could not mess up our perfect makeup. It took too long to apply it on and we were at the train station. We dabbed each others eyes. Reapplied our lipstick and grinned with love for each other.

Instinctively I took her hand and squeezed it. "I love you so," I said. Virginia replied, "And I love you too."

At that moment old # 6 was making its way around the curve, before it stopped at the train station. The smoke billowed from the engine and we knew the camp cars were trailing behind. The excitement increased as the train began to slow. It slowly came to a halt as Virginia and I stood in front of the camp cars. The door opened and this time it is Ben in the front with Joe at his heels. The guys didn't take the steps. They jumped straight from the train and into our arms. Ben hugged me tightly as he swung me around. He smelled so good and felt so wonderful! I was thrilled beyond my wildest dreams being in his arms once again. He kissed me passionately, slowly and then more intensely. He held me close with his breath upon my neck. I felt deliriously happy. "Aura Leigh, Aura Leigh," he kept saying my name over and over. "I knew you'd forgive me. I knew you'd come back to me," Ben whispered.

"I love you Ben." I said without any doubt that this was true. From the first moment I laid eyes on you, I loved you.

Chapter Thirteen

Graduation had come and gone and time seemed to pass quickly. Virginia stayed in Flannery and I had gotten a job in a nearby town. I stayed with my sister Gayetta and her husband. Gayetta worked hard in her home and it was as clean as Mama's. She was such a fine woman and a good cook. She seemed happy with her life. It was a good feeling living with Gayetta again. In her cozy little two bedroom house, she and husband John worked side by side.

John was a stocky built man with good looks and a magnetic personality. When he gave you a hug, you knew you were hugged. He welcomed me with both of those strong arms.

I worked hard and saved my money in the days ahead. I had plans-big plans. Ben worked hard too. The faster we saved our money, the faster we could rent us a house and get married.

Being a waitress was not an easy job, I found out. People were very picky. Sometimes their coffee was too hot. Sometimes it was not hot enough. The presentation of food seemed to never look nice enough. It was as if people would stir their food up in a pile and then say, "I can't eat this mess!"

I remember one day in particular. It was hot as hell this August afternoon. The fans in the restaurant were working overtime, just to blow this hot air and cigarette smoke around the room. A couple had eaten their dinner without hesitation. I asked them if they would like dessert. The balding fat man said, "Yes, I would like a chocolate sundae." "Okay," I said as I walked off.

It was a very busy day, and tempers were short, with all these people as they breathed and sweated in the small restaurant. The women sipped on their drinks, fanned themselves, and tried hard to look presentable in the heat. I fixed the chocolate sundae and took it to my customers table. He took one bite of the sundae (which was melting from all the heat) and said, "Here lady, take it back, I don't want to drink the damn thing!"

I was so mad! I just looked at my customer and said, "Looks good to me." I took the sundae. Using his spoon, I dove into the drizzled chocolate and the melting ice-cream. I got a large amount on his spoon and took a great big bite. "Tastes good too," I stated. The couple's mouths just dropped open with amazement as I marched off. At that moment I realized what I had done. For a minute I thought I was going to be sick, just thinking of eating after that man. Then, I decided I was so hot and tired, I just didn't care. I kept eating that sundae all the way to the kitchen!

As the days went by, I just about wore out the door that opened and closed my sister's mailbox. I would check and recheck for Ben's letters. How exciting it was when the letters came.. Each letter from Ben was invaluable. I knew that Ben had touched it. The words on each page came from his heart. How I missed him so and ached for his touch.

Finally, the letter of all letters came. Ben would be coming in to work in Flannery in two weeks. He would work a four day week and then would be off for three days. Ben said that he and Joe had been in a big poker game and had won. He found a place for us about an hour away from Flannery to rent. He had taken his poker money and paid for it! He didn't say what it looked like so I used my imagination. He wanted us to get married when he came to town…

I held the letter in my hand then kissed it and cried. My waiting and loneliness would be over. Finally, I'd be out of this hellacious job. I would be married to Ben and live happily ever after. I stood at the mailbox, hanging onto it for support. I wonder what my new home with Ben would look like. Would it have the claw foot tub and sink I wanted? I pictured this wonderful home in my mind. It would have white with gray steps leading to the porch. The living room would have a colorful couch with dark end tables and starched doilies that Mama would make for me. Our bedroom would have pale blue wallpaper. In the corner would be a dark mahogany chest with matching bed. Straight across from the foot of the bed would be our dresser, complete with large round mirror. I blushed when I thought of all the mirror would see with Ben and I in the bed night after night. What would our first night be like? I had imagined it time and time again. Ben's wonderful, strong hands would be on me. He had been with other women and knew a woman's needs. This I did not doubt. This probably would make another girl jealous. I guess in a way it did me too. On the other hand, it made me feel strangely secure. I had never made love to a man. With all the emotions that flooded my soul when Ben kissed and touched me, I knew the journey would be one that I would never forget. Seasoned hands, that's Ben had and I liked it. As I held tightly to my letter that holds my future in it, I ran into the house to show my beautiful sister Gayetta, and left the tired mailbox door hanging open.

Chapter Fourteen

It was good to be home in Flannery again. I noticed flowers of all colors and sizes surrounding our lovely, shiny gray porch. As I walked in the door, I noticed that the house, as usual, was so clean you could eat off the floors. All of us girls were grown and Leanna was the only one of us living at home. The house was quieter than I had remembered.

Leanna was a senior in high school. She was doing her homework sitting on the couch with pencil in hand. As she saw me walk in, pencil and papers were thrown aside. She ran and threw both arms around my neck. "Oh Aura Leigh, it is so good to see you!" she said.

Tears ran down my cheeks as I hugged my baby sister, "It is wonderful to see you too." I said as I held her close. She was beautiful with her dark, wavy hair down about her shoulders. Even though we were all pretty girls, I felt that Leanna was the prettiest. Her complexion was flawless, with a smile that could stop someone in their tracks. She didn't seem to know it, though. There was a kind of insecurity about her that had lasted her whole life. I wonder what would cause such a beautiful girl to be so insecure.

"Oh my God," Mama said wistfully when she saw me. "Aura Leigh, You've come home!" she cried. What a wonderful hug Mama gave me. I just breathed her in. How good it felt to be hugged by this woman. The security in her embrace made me feel like everything was alright- better than alright. It was perfect! I thought that it was God's gift to have Mamas that made you feel that way. It was better than a birthday or Christmas. It was the most complete feeling that could ever be. Being loved by a woman such as my Mama - No greater gift could one ever receive.

We sat in Mama's kitchen. Fresh hot coffee to drink along with a piece of Mama's apple pie was a perfect start to telling my story… "Ben is coming to Flannery in less than a week and a half! He has found us a house to rent and wants to marry me when he comes in!"

Leanna squealed with excitement! "He is sooo cute Aura Leigh," Leanna said with that beautiful smile broadening.

Mama placed her soft hand upon mine. "Are you sure this is what you want?" Mama said calmly while looking into my eyes.

"Yes Mama, with all my heart and soul, yes," I replied softly.

"Marriage is not easy in the best of circumstances," Mama began. "It is give and take on both sides. I know when you think about it, Aura Leigh, you find it a wonderful place where all you dreams will be fulfilled and it can be that at times. But most of the time it takes work to make a marriage a good one. You will have hard times and babies. You will do without a lot of things at first. You need to support your man and work side by side with him. Love him with all your heart and talk everything out. Don't go to bed mad, Aura Leigh. Solve your problems before bed and then hold him close at night. A man needs that, just as a woman does."

"Oh Mama, I promise I will take your words to heart and do the best I can with them," I replied. Mama smiled a kind of sad loving smile that I had not ever seen before.

In years to come, there will be many times that I will look back and recall this look of my Mama's.

"We can't plan a wedding on such short notice Aura Leigh," Mama began. "I can make you a white dress from whatever pattern you choose, but we will have to get started right away. We could get preacher Jennings to marry ya'll," she went on.

"Oh Mama," I began crying. Partly because I knew that I would never be a child anymore. I no longer would have my bed where I could look out of the window and make wishes. My home, my Mamas home would be a place to visit, not to live. How many happy memories were in this house for me? Too numerous to count, I was sure. The security of home, the only home I had ever known would change. Such a momentary sadness came upon me. I quickly brushed it away before anyone could see.

"Ok, we will pick out a pattern today Mama," I said. I have got to call Virginia! What a wonderful thought. Virginia! How much I loved her, I couldn't imagine. I excused myself quickly from the kitchen. I ran to the phone and called her number. Virginia…

Chapter Fifteen

The streets of Flannery were bustling as Virginia and I came to town. There were old men sitting in front of the barber shop with newspapers in hand. They just held them without reading while in deep conversation about the people who were walking up and down the sidewalk. It made you wonder why they had the papers in the first place.

We passed the drugstore where Virginia and I once hid our books in the grass to get a sundae. It seemed so long ago when we looked out that window and we saw the camp cars. We surely could not have imagined that the one day we laid out of school would change our lives completely. It was a wonderful memory looking back on the way we met Ben and Joe. I saw Virginia's pretty freckled face and knew she was remembering the same thing. We squeezed each other's hand and took off running to the five and ten cents store.

Inside it seemed like half the town's women were there. They were all looking at dress patterns. We nudged our way through the crowd. They made frowns and breathed hard at us saying, "Well" like we had committed a crime. "It's not every day that two women are getting married," I said with a big grin. The women's' frowns turned to smiles as one said, "My daughter just got married and I made her dress!" She was a plump, short woman with silver hair that was twisted up in the back with clear combs. She had made her daughter a white dress with blue flowers on it and a matching belt. I felt sure she had made her dress and had done a fine job with it. Virginia and I needed all the help we could get, we decided.

"That's the one right there" the lady said as she pointed to a certain pattern. It was a white dress that was a little off the shoulders and had a plunging neckline. It had lots of satin buttons going down the back and a small, white belt to match. It looked tight which would show off my curves. The low neckline would accentuate my large bust.

I hugged the older woman tightly. "Thank you so much!," I exclaimed. "You have picked the perfect dress for me." Virginia smiled that sweet smile. I knew that she liked the dress pattern as well. "Ok Virginia, your turn."

She picked a beautiful pattern. The dress was cut in a straight line above the bust to fit snuggly, which enhanced Virginia's wonderful figure. The bolero jacket would be worn over the dress with belt.

We exchanged lots of tearful hugs as we took our patterns and material and stepped into the cab. The ride home was more subdued. We were lost in our thoughts of the changes that would soon take place. Never would we ride together alone in a cab again.

Chapter Sixteen

The leaves on the trees were a myriad of colors. With the sun shining down through them, it reminded me of a rainbow.

I lay in my bed this one last morning with such a feeling of happiness, it was hard to put into words. All of my hopes and dreams were finally coming true. Ben would be mine and I his. Everything was all set. The preacher would marry all four of us at 2p.m. today, this 21st day of October, 1947.

I knew Virginia must be feeling all the happy feelings that I was. It's truly amazing how in a days time, your life could be completely and forever changed. I would be married. I would no longer be a virgin. How I stayed one this long is just beyond me! It's not that Ben and I haven't been close. My goodness, there were times I thought that we wouldn't stop. He had such warm kisses that started with my mouth and moved quickly to my neck. It just seemed to be the natural thing to do. His hard body would press against mine. I could feel his hands all over me. I knew that tonight would be something I could never forget.

We were going to Pinewalk for our honeymoon. Virginia and I had always dreamed of going to Pinewalk, and now we were! It was just like on our first date with Ben and Joe- a cab would be picking us up. It was the town of one-way streets! My sister, Gayetta had gone there when she was married. She talked about what a lively town it was. I could just see it in my mind's eye: The restaurants, cars whizzing by and street lights. Everything that Flannery didn't have.

Sure, we had our drug store and the five and ten. It was just a small country town. I had never been out of this town far enough to make a difference. Just the thought sent a smile clear through me. Soon we would see a totally new life and we'd come back married women. We'd know what it was like to be loved both mentally and physically. The thought of Ben's skin next to mine; A rush of excitement went through me to my very core.

I smelled the wonderful food Mama had prepared making its way up to my bed. It was calling me to breakfast. So blessed I have been, right down to good food from my Mama's table.

When I got out of bed, I saw my beautiful wedding dress hanging on the closet door, and it beckoned me. Impulsively, I ran over and hugged it. Every detail of my dress was perfect. Each little white, satin button was perfectly in line and going down the back of my dress. It was made lovingly just for me. I could hardly breathe from all the happiness I felt inside. I just may burst!

Chapter Seventeen

"Help me, Aura Leigh," Virginia said as she attempted to pin her hat to her beautiful red hair. Her hair was swept up neatly in back with a silver comb. The front had a small amount of bangs gathered to one side. Virginia's hat was secured with a short white veil that extended over her eyes. Her jacket was in complete harmony with her lovely white dress. We both wore rose colored lipstick. It seemed to match perfectly for us. What a beautiful bride you are, Virginia! "And you as well," Virginia stated matter of fact.

My dress was a perfect fit. It had just enough cleavage to make Ben desire me, however not too much to make me look cheap. I swept my hair up with a flowered comb. "I don't think we have ever looked better, Virginia," I laughed a nervous laugh and we hugged.

"You are right, Aura Leigh."

As we walked down the aisle, Virginia held her father's arm; I held the arm of John (my sister Gayettas' husband), who was giving me away. I Looked around at the small gathering of family and friends and felt so many feelings. All of my sisters were sitting in pews with their husbands. Leanna was the exception, though there were plenty of suitors that fought for her attention.

She was so beautiful although somehow, she never realized this. She was an outgoing young woman; however, her insecurities always seemed to show. She sat up front at the old church piano, her black hair perfectly in place.

Sister Dianna and Sister Hannah, of course, sat side by side on their pew with their husbands sitting beside them. They had always done everything together. I imagine they are each other's best friend as well as sisters. I wonder what kind of life each of them had now. They had both always been so quiet and shy. I was glad they had each other to lean on. Was it my imagination or did Dianne's husband appear cold and unfeeling? No smile had I seen pass between her and her guy. He didn't offer an arm around this pretty, fragile girl. Dianne could have just as well been sitting alone. The girls looked so small next to their men. Both seemed shy and withdrawn, though, both girls were so pretty, yet, they had an appearance of empty shells. No excitement, just blank faces, which gave nothing away. My heart could not have had a clue, for I'd never known a life such as theirs.

I would soon learn many things that I would never have wanted to know- to accept. What a roll of the dice for me and my sisters. If one could look into the future and see the lives we would have, would we have made different choices?

I was too happy living my own dream, now, coming true. Gayetta watching her man walk me down the aisle showing a sense of pride on her face. She squeezed Mama's hand as a tear slips down Mama's cheek. Mama looked so small as she sat on the pew amongst the family. Her two piece beige suit pressed neatly. Mama's eyes caught mine as I continued down the aisle. Was it a hint of concern I saw in them? In a flash, I looked at them again. This time they were filled only with love for me.

As I looked about this small church, I saw the people who had known me from the time I was a child. They had helped raise and guide me into the woman I am. Today, they will see me take my first steps as a wife. Leanna grinned from ear to ear as she played the piano. She gave me a small wink as we proceeded down the aisle.

As I looked down the aisle, I saw the preacher, Ben and Joe. How handsome they both were. Joe had his dark hair perfectly in place and his dark suit to match. Ben- my Ben stood beside him, with his sandy hair and his tan suit on. I became oblivious to everyone else once Ben's eyes met mine. They looked at me approvingly as they looked down to my cleavage. I felt warmth flood my very soul with his look. He knew he would soon have me body and soul. As I took a stand by his side, Ben's eyes rose from my body and began to look into mine. There was so much emotion in those eyes. Somewhere in a distance, as if it were coming from a long tunnel, I heard: Dearly beloved…

Chapter Eighteen

We were all giddy as the taxi cab as it took the four of us to Pinewalk. The guys playfully poked each other from time to time with that knowing look. It would not be long until our lives would change forever. Being virgins, Virginia and I had only imagined and talked about what it would feel like to have the man of our dreams inside of us. How many nights had Virginia spent the night with me? We'd lie in my wonderful bed with our night gowns on; we'd look out the window. We'd plan our life as we gazed at the stars. She and I would talk about this very night. The night we would be married. We solved many a problem lying in that large, soft feather bed. It was nice being young girls and the wonder of all that is. The imagining of what life held in store for us. I would look back and miss this time in my life.

Ben's arm was about my shoulder with his hand resting on my arm. His fingers would travel softly about, dancing lovingly above my breast. I could only imagine what he would be doing without Joe and Virginia beside us. After all, I was his now, body and soul for the taking. I was ready. The stirring his fingers made deep within me told me so.

The cab finally pulled up to the large, white Hotel. The guys stood at the car's window. Putting their money together, they paid the driver. Ben's jacket thrown over his shoulder, top buttons on his white shirt were unbuttoned. A strand of his sandy, blonde hair hung softly on his forehead. This made him look even more handsome. Virginia and I stood back in eager anticipation. She put her arm around me and hugged me with delight. Joe walked quickly over to Virginia and pulled her close to him as he grinned from ear to ear. Ben quickly followed. He picked me up and twirled me around. He then stopped and let my body slide slowly down his as he held me tightly pressed to him. A low moan escaped me before I had a moment to catch it. He kissed me with a long, penetrating kiss. I felt weak and dizzy and at the same time, so alive. I glanced over at Joe and Virginia. They were oblivious to us. We all walked up the steps and onto a large, blue wooden porch towards the screen door.

As we walked into the hotel, I couldn't help but marvel how large the lobby was! The walls had thin, white, horizontal boards rising high into the air to a tall ceiling. I just knew it would echo if I were to yell. There was a large set of stairs to the right of the counter where the guys paid for our rooms. We proceeded up those large, wooden stairs, all the while I thought, "This is the last set of stairs I will ever climb as a virgin." I looked down after we reached the top. How far I had come from the young girl I once was. I could never go back, not that I wanted to. Ben interrupted my thoughts with a kiss on my neck. "Let's go," he said in a low voice. The key turned the lock to our room…

Chapter Nineteen

The days rolled by quickly as Ben, Joe, Virginia and I walked the streets of Pinewalk. It was like a wonderful dream. The days were full of sunshine and the leaves on the trees were alive with a vast array of autumn colors. The gentle breeze caused the leaves to randomly float to the ground. Down from our hotel was the Big Shady River. We took two row boats and set off. The river was calm and beautiful. Joe and Virginia's boat drifted to the left as the river branched off. Ben's arms looked so strong as he rowed effortlessly. The river was quiet and no other boat appeared on the water. Ben rowed until the bottom of the gray, wooden boat slid on the dirt below. We had rowed to the right side of the river's edge. Thick trees ran alongside the embankment. The long branches had thick, colorful leaves that draped themselves over top of our boat. This created a wonderful shade from the sun. Ben laid the oars down and walked over to where I sat. "You're rocking the boat," I said with a grin. Ben looked into my eyes as he sat down. "That's just what I plan to do," he said with a wink and pulled me close to him.

As we lay curled up in the bottom of the boat, I am thinking out loud. "I don't care if we ever leave this boat." "The feeling of your body next to mine outside and in a boat… they just don't make words to describe this Ben," I said quietly as I snuggled more closely. Our clothes were tossed about and a small blanket was draped over us. We were quiet for awhile as we enjoyed complete satisfaction as the sun began to set. Never had I felt such so calm and relaxed. The cool of the evening had begun to settle in. Reluctantly, we dressed and Ben started rowing us back towards our hotel.

The wonderful love that Ben and I shared the next few days was amazing. What a wonderful lover he was. Though I had never known another, I felt sure he had to be the best. He was so tender and so patient as he made love to me. He wanted me to feel as much joy as he felt and I was sure I did. It was wonderful to sleep beside Ben. To lay my head on his chest at night and hear his heart beat, a heart that loved only me. I knew I was the luckiest girl in the world. If I moved or turned away, he would wake. He would find me and our loving would start over and over again. With each kiss, each caress brought me to a place I could never have imagined. I could not see anything beyond Ben. He was now my life. I wanted to please him in every way that I could. Virginia and Joe seemed so happy also. Though we were together throughout the day, eating in the small café or walking along the river, they never took their eyes off of one another.

The taxi all too soon came and picked us up. Though I did not know it then, I would never go back there again. I looked out the back window and watched the large hotel and the wonderful town fade until it was out of sight. It was etched forever in my memory of this wonderful time we shared. I would replay it over and over again. This was the happiest time in my life. I would never again be as happy as I was at that moment.

We were returning home. I had not seen our house that Ben has rented for us. With the honeymoon and everything going so fast, I had not room in my mind to really think about the house that he and I would share. I was sure that if Ben rented it, the home would be wonderful. It was a little more than an hour away from my hometown of Flannery; we would be living in a place called Coalwood. We were on our way and I would soon know. The cab stopped and Joe and Virginia got out.

They were staying with Joe's family until they got a place of their own. Virginia bent her head back into the back seat and reached her hand out and squeezed mine. "I love you so, Virginia," I said. A tear rolled down my cheek, as I reached up and brushed it away.

We promised we would see each other soon and we would surely write. There was no phone number to share. Ben and I didn't have a phone yet, since he just got the place. I was sure we'd have one soon. I was so sure of a lot of things.

The ride to our new home held lots of emotions. We were both quiet; however, my mind was anything but quiet. I would be living away from my Mama, my home and Virginia. Everything I had ever known would be in another place. This was certainly an unfamiliar feeling to me. In my core, I felt certain homesickness. I quickly tried to dismiss this, for I was now Ben's wife. I was a seventeen year old woman. I should not feel this emptiness and longing for my Mama, for the smell of home. It was such a clean and wonderful place to be. Everything fell into place there. What kind of wife would I be? What would Ben expect of me? What kind of husband would he be? I looked up at my husband who seemed to be having his own thoughts as he quietly looked out the window. I shook off my fears and reassured myself that all was wonderful. I loved Ben. I loved him enough to move from my family. He was my family now. We will build a wonderful life together. I will have his children. I lay my head on his chest and hugged him closely. His arms wrapped around me and his mouth searched and found mine. All was well.

Chapter Twenty

We traveled a long winding road that lead to our new home. The day was almost over and night had begun to fall as the taxi traveled this narrow and rough road. There were many holes and ridges which made the ride unsettling to my stomach.

The car finally came to a halt. Ben paid the driver and he helped me out of the car. We got our suitcases as I looked up. It was almost dark; however, I could still see where I was going. There was what appeared to be an old, rusty chicken fence that surrounded the small yard. Ben opened the rickety gate which seemed to be half off its hinges. I silently walked through the gate first. The grass and weeds were sparse, yet rose up my leg and at times, reached my thighs. With my pretty yellow, button down dress and sweater on along complete with high heeled shoes, this was quite a challenge simply to wade through.

Just ahead was a small, wooden house. It appeared old and unpainted. The steps were uneven. Ben, with a suitcase in his left hand, took his right hand and held my arm for stability as I attempted to climb the stairs. There was no lock on the door. He opened the door and I walked in. "Where's the light switch," I asked?

"Just a minute," Ben said. He struck a match and lit the oil lamp that was positioned on the wall. Through the dim, yellow light, I looked around at my two room home. I was in disbelief, though I hoped it didn't show on my face. No bathroom, no clawfoot tub like I had planned for my home so long ago in home-ec class. No electricity, no running water. There was a faded blue couch and chair in the living room. A pot bellied black stove with four legs sat by the chair.

Ben ran outside to a coal pile at the edge of the yard. I held my sweater tightly with both hands as I felt a chill run down my spine. In a few minutes Ben walked back in with the coal bucket. It was filled to the top with shiny, black coal. He placed the lumps of coal into the pot bellied stove. While he was getting a fire going in that pot bellied stove, I continued to look around.

On the opposite side of the living room, there stood an old kitchen table and four chairs. The wooden table looked tired. It sure could use a good painting, I thought. A gray, metal pail with a ladle resting inside was sitting on the kitchen Table. It was there for us to drink water from.

There was a small cupboard and an old coal cook stove that stood by the back door. I opened the cupboard slowly. You never knew what might come out of a cabinet that hasn't been opened for awhile. There were a few dishes on the shelves and silver ware in the drawer. An old broom sat quietly by the door in waiting. I was sure it was waiting for me. There was no door, just a doorway that separated our bedroom from our living room and kitchen area.

The bedroom had a metal framed bed with gray striped mattress. A chest of drawers sat across the room from the bed. A wash bowl and picture sat on top of it. The home smelled of dampness and dust. Ben mentioned that there was bedding in the chest of drawers. With the pale light that shined quietly from the living room, I found a sheet and a couple of blankets, two pillows. I slowly made the bed.

My mind really couldn't register this new life. It was very unfamiliar and I wasn't sure what to even say to Ben. I made the bed nice and neat while Ben had the pot bellied stove fire going.

There was a small window on the stove with vertical vents on the side that you could see through to the blue and yellow flames. This lit up the home and made the living room much more inviting. Warmth came to the small house quickly. Ben took the metal pail outside and came back with cool, clear water in it. He said there was a spring to the left side of our yard where we could easily get our water. He dipped the ladle into the water and gave me a drink. The cold water tasted so good on my tongue. I didn't realize that I was parched. This was partly because of the long drive, and partly because of the shock of where I was. I drank the water down quickly. Ben laughed and put the ladle down. I looked at him and felt a better sense of security settle in. He would take care of me, I thought. I smiled easily at him and he held me close. Before I knew it, Ben picked me up. He carried me to our bed. The fire from the stove flickered across the cover. Ben's love enveloped me.

Chapter Twenty One

I awoke to the sunshine beaming through the window and straight for my eyes. As they slowly opened, I began to focus on this unfamiliar room. The window was so dirty, I wondered how the sun could have possible made its way into the room. I stretched and rolled over to face my husband. He was already out of the bed and in the next room. What a wonderful aroma filled the air. The smell of bacon and eggs! I realized I hadn't eaten since yesterday in Pinewalk. I was starving!

I quickly threw back the blankets, slipped my shoes on and put on my robe. The house was nice and warm. The old potbellied stove made a crackling sound. As I walked over to Ben, he was oblivious to me. Facing the stove, he was busy frying eggs on the old cookstove. The fire from the coal inside of the stove radiated out with intense heat. Ben turned to me and gave me a wonderful hug.

"Ben, where did you get bacon and eggs?" I asked.

"There's a country store just around the curve in the road Aura Leigh." Ben went on. "They have lots of food there. They have a lot of things."

I was so grateful to know this. I hadn't really thought about how we would eat, however, that would have been on my mind very soon.

Ben had gotten our washbowl full of warm water (heated on the stove) and a hand towel on the back of the chair. I washed my hands and face and began washing the table. I set our plates and silverware down and Ben had a pot of coffee on the stove. It was perking and the smell of fresh, rich coffee filled the air. I poured two cups of coffee and Ben served the eggs and bacon.

The taste of the food was wonderful, along with the warm cup of coffee. It almost made me forget for the moment where I was and how we would we survive here.

Ben started the conversation. "Aura Leigh, I know you were used to having electricity, a phone and a beautiful farm. I promise that I will get you a wonderful home real soon. This is just temporary. We can fix this place up, in the meantime. Why, a little paint and some mowing, this place will be ok. We have that little spring outside, Aura Leigh. The landlord said it has never run dry. We can set our milk and cold stuff in there and it will stay nice and cool. There is a scrub board and two wash pans outback in the yard for the wash. I will put up a nice clothes line for us and I will help all I can. I so look forward to coming home after work just to be with you, my darling. Just to feel you next to me and know that you are mine. What a lucky man I am."

He smiled and gave me a wonderful kiss. I held him close, he smelled so wonderful. "Where's my dessert?" Ben said as he pulled me close to him.

At night our love was so special. I could not see him clearly, though I could feel him beside me. By day, love had a new meaning. To be able to see Ben as he brought me to heights I could never have fantasized about. I didn't have to wonder (with the bright sunshine streaming in the window) where he would kiss me and travel about my body, I could watch. There was something so erotic about this. The pleasure peaks and then we lie quietly, facing one another. Ben reached up and brushed a strand of hair back from my face. "You are an amazing woman, Aura Leigh," Ben said quietly and kissed my nose.

"Hmmm," I said. That's about all I could say. After a few minutes Ben started talking. "When I get to work full time on the railroad, we will move into a wonderful home, with a bathroom and running water."

That was all I needed to hear. He had a plan. I was a hard worker like my Mama. I could do this. I had to. I reached and gave him a quick kiss. "Let's get busy," I said, "if we are going to make this house our home."

We walked hand in hand down to the old store. There was a wonderful heavyset woman behind the counter named Betty, who worked there. She helped us with paint, nails, food and even some old curtains she had in the back room. The little store did have a little bit of everything. I could walk down and visit this woman, when I was lonely and Ben was at work. It'll all work out.

The next few days we truly made the small house our home. Ben used an old push mower and pushed, pulled and mowed down the grass and weeds. He nailed and fixed the old rickety steps. He put a hinge on the old rusty gate. He even placed a piece of rectangular wood on the inside of the front and back door with a nail in the center. You turned it and no one can get into your home. A cheap lock it was- just like the one in our out house at home. It did make me feel better.

Me, well I washed curtains, starched and ironed them, cleaned the windows and hung the curtains up. I painted the kitchen table a tan color. I swept and mopped the old plank floor. I took the couch cushions outside and beat the dust off with a broom. I must say the kitchen coal stove was shiny and clean. It was truly hard to keep things clean with coal heat. It gave off heat as well as something we called soot.

Little specks of black coal particles would float and land on you, the furniture, and the floor. It was a daily chore just keeping the dust off everything.

The outhouse was on the right side of the house. The wooden boards had shrunk up over the years. Through the large cracks, you could see out pretty easily while you were doing your business. I thought to myself, it's a good thing there's not many close neighbors. If they walked up, they could peer in and here I'd be.

I kept our clothes washed and the clothes line Ben hung for me was very sturdy. He was very handy with fixing things. Together we were a good team. The days were filled with a lot of work and I wasn't a very good cook. That's the one thing Mama and the older sisters did well. They kept us younger sisters out of the kitchen; however, we did more than our share of house work. Now, I am trying to cook for my man. He's very kind and bragged on some things that no one else, in their right mind, would eat. I made a chocolate pie one night. It looked so pretty with the meringue piled high. Ben loved dessert and I knew he had been anticipating this pie. He cut a slice and the pie ran like chocolate milk all over his plate. I started to cry, for I had worked so hard on this pie. He quickly chased the thin pie around his plate and scooped it into his mouth. "Aura Leigh, best pie I ever ate," he grinned. This made me love him all the more. He was a much better cook than I, but he never said a thing about it.

In the evening, we'd sit out on the steps with Ben's guitar in hand. I would lean against the porch and enjoy his voice and the melody of his guitar. He'd sing awhile and I'd join in. Sometimes a neighbor would hear us and walk over, sit, and listen. This made the house seem more like home. Sometimes we'd sit and plan our future on those steps. We had wonderful talks and the loving at the end of the day. No wonder, within the first month, I was pregnant.

Chapter Twenty Two

Winter came and snowed us in. Ben worked every chance he got. He'd come home sometimes with his coveralls frozen to his legs and icicles hanging off, yet he never complained. When he was home, he'd help out with any of the housework. Letters came from Mama and Virginia. I cherished each and every word. It was my lifeline to a life that seemed to be fading. Virginia and Joe were very happy. They had gotten a home in Flannery. Mama said Leanna were fine. She had undertones in her letter that led me to believe something was not quite right about Leanna. I dismissed it after Mama went on to say my baby sister had eloped with a local boy named CJ. He was an attractive guy, as I remember. A real ladies man... I didn't think Mama liked him, by the feeling I got from her letter. She mentioned my older sisters Hannah and Diane. She said Hanna had been depressed some and Diane had been trying to help her. I thought to myself, how could depressed person help another, though I would never write this back to Mama. She seemed happy, yet reserved about me being pregnant. Mama had a truthful way about her. You could tell if something wasn't quite right with her. I wrote her back and told her that Ben's sister Violet lived here in Coalwood as well as his mother. She said she would be here to help me deliver this little one. She said she had done it dozens of times.

Ben grew up in this town in a small, four room house. You had to walk way up into a holler to get to it.... He had talked about not having shoes to wear as a boy. He'd be on his way to school and see a bunch of cows resting on the ground. He'd run the cows off and stood where they were lying just to warm his feet…

Finally, we went to visit Ben's family. The house was small and full of love and laughter. His mother was a wonderful cook using her coal stove. She had no electricity either. She could make the best cornbread and roast beef that I had ever eaten. It was so tender; you didn't even have to chew, hardly. He had four older brothers and two sisters, one older and one younger. The brothers were all stunningly handsome, like Ben. His sisters were very open and friendly. Ben's mother was very good to me. More than one time, she'd catch the train and ride across town just to bring me kindling. (This was small pieces of wood to get my fire started.) She brought canned vegetables and jams. This helped us get through the tough winter.

Yes, his family loved me from the very start and I them. It was nice being part of Ben's family. His daddy also worked on the railroad. He was a short, stocky, and quiet man, however, when he spoke, he meant every word. A few years back he had been unfaithful to Ben's mother and she eventually found out. She was a strong, country woman and true to her convictions. Though some sort of forgiveness may have settled in, there was a distance between them that you could feel. They, however, lived together in peace.

I remember his older sister was quite a story teller. You could sit for hours and listen to her talk. Sometimes she would tell ghost stories and I would get pretty scared. The shadows on the wall would get longer. The outside would get darker and I sure wouldn't go to the outhouse alone. His sisters would laugh at me, however, they would take my hand and walk with me to the outside toilet. I felt this saved me from the dark shadows of the holler.

Chapter Twenty Three

I'd been having contractions all day. Ben had gotten his sister Violet over and she had cooked and kept the house while I seemed to have one pain and then another. She said this was common and nothing to worry about. I would take turns walking, sitting and then finally lying in bed. My pain became intense. I so wished I had my Mama, the hospital in Flannery, my sisters. I began crying out with pain. An hour had passed, two three, fifteen hours of contractions and nothing. "I want my mother!" I screamed. Ben held my hand and a concerned look was on his face. It'll be ok, Ben said as he held me in his arms. I pushed away. I felt as if I could not breathe. I felt as if something wasn't right. Ben and his sister began whispering. Through all the pain I could not make out what they had said.

Finally, his sister checked me. "Breech birth," she said.

"What the hell does that mean!" I shouted.

She ignored me and told Ben to tie a sheet to the bottom of the bed. She just tied a knot to the end of the sheet. She said, "Aura Leigh, when I tell you to, then bite down on this knot." She told Ben to hold my hand. "Aura Leigh, squeeze Ben's hand and bite down on your knot!" She yelled. I did just what she said. She was checking the insides of me. I felt a huge turning motion in my belly; I bit down on the knot in the sheet while I squeezed Ben's hand until I thought I might have broken it. As the tears streamed down my face, a deep yell from the core of me rang out. "Oh God help me!" I cried. I felt cold and clammy with beads of sweat appearing on my face. "Now," Violet continued, "that baby is in the right position."

It was a good thing I couldn't see below my enlarged belly at the puddle of blood she left after turning my baby. She walked over to the wash basin and washed the blood off of her hands.

The rest of the evening was a blur- the screaming with contractions, the intense pain. Twenty six hours total had gone and I began to tug on the sheet with all of my might! "That's the way," said Violet and with one last pain came the baby's cry.

"It's a boy," Violet said as she took him and washed him up. Ben wrapped the baby in a blanket and held it a moment. What a beautiful sight to see. The man that I love was holding our son with so much love in his eyes. He brought him over and laid him beside me. What a head full of black hair, just like mine I thought. He was beautiful. I opened the blue blanket to look at my precious son. He was so handsome with smooth, soft skin. I counted ten fingers and ten toes. Knowing my son was ok, I fell into a good, long and needed sleep.

Violet stayed with us and helped me with chores until the baby and I got stronger. I was so grateful. She had children and a husband of her own, yet she stayed with me. There was no way you could repay someone for such kindness. So the day came and she was gone and there was Ben, the baby and I. We had chosen the name Ethan. It was a strong, handsome name. I was sure that was what Ethan would grow up to be.

Chapter Twenty Four

Ethan was nine months old and walking from Ben to me. Such a young age for walking, yet he was so strong. His beautiful black hair and olive skin made him one of the handsomest boys I'd ever seen. When we'd go to the little store, people would gather around Ethan. He never saw a stranger. They were just drawn to him. And Ben- he was so proud of him and took such an active role as a father. Ben would come in from work at night, give me a kiss and Ethan would run to his dad. The two would play for hours. The bond they had was a wonderful sight to see.

It was a warm night in May. All was quiet when we lay down to sleep. Ethan was sleeping quietly in his crib that stood beside our bed. We awoke with a startle around one in the morning. Ethan was crying loudly. Ben jumped and picked his son up. He held him, cradled him, and nothing helped. I walked with him, I tried to feed him. This went on for hours and finally Ben left Ethan and me. He walked to the store and called a taxi. Soon after, he returned with loving sister Violet. There was no consoling our son. I could not imagine what could be wrong. He was such a happy and good natured baby.

Violet took one look at Ethan and said we needed to get him to the hospital. By this time he was warm to the touch and sweaty. We went back down to the store to use the phone and all the while Ethan has been screaming and arching his back in an odd sort of way. I called my mother and she agreed to meet us at the hospital.

The doctor at the country hospital said he was going to have to do a spinal tap. I had no clue what that even was. I walked and held my crying son. I was at my wit's end. I began to cry uncontrollably. Ben took the baby and Mama walked me out of the room. I stayed outside the room during the procedure. All the while I could here Ethan scream and cry. Ben stayed in the room to hold him. Mama sat with me and held my hand. She offered up a beautiful prayer. My mother-she was the strongest woman I have ever known. I was so glad she had come to be with me. We sat for what seemed to be an eternity. Ethan had quit crying and all was calm. After a good bit of time had passed, Mama got up and went into the room with Ben, the doctor and Ethan. I stayed out and prayed and prayed. Dear God, please deliver my son from whatever this is. Please let us get back to our life. He's such a special little boy dear God. Over and over I wrung my hands, prayed and cried… I felt as if my prayers just hit the ceiling and floated back down to me… The silence suddenly felt unbearable.

Mama was the first one out of the room. She said, "The Lord giveth and the Lord taketh away—blessed be the name of the Lord."

I do not remember the rest of that day. I learned later that Ethan died in Ben's arms with a disease called meningitis. Ethan was buried in an unmarked grave. We had no money for a marker; just a wooden cross to mark my baby's grave.

Mama stayed with Ben and me for the next few weeks. I do not remember much of this time. I was down in a hole and to climb out seemed near impossible. Ben had his own grief. His son was dead. We were like walking strangers and Mama fed us and kept the house going for the next few weeks.

Little did I know that Mama was not only carrying around the burden for the loss of her grandson, but both of my sisters Hanna and Diane were not doing well. Depressed beyond reason, the doctor said. Hannah's husband was supportive of her and took good care of their daughter. Diane's husband left her with three small little girls. Dianne couldn't cope and ended up in a mental hospital. The three children were soon adopted out. Mother was also trying to help Leanna out of the mess she was in with CJ. He was physically abusive and a drunk. My little mother had such a lot on her plate. She did not dare tell me this for a long time. She knew with my fragile state of mind, I could not have handled any more grief.

Slowly, over the next several months, I climbed out of my depression. Ben was working more and we had moved into a four room house with electricity. We even had a bathroom. We slowly rekindled some of the love that had been set aside during this tragedy. We began playing and laughing again… And loving…What a wonderful gift we had there….and then…..I again was pregnant.

The joy at the thought of another child thrilled Ben. He kissed me and kissed me upon finding out. We laughed and began to plan. I had one uncomfortable feeling though. Ben kept talking about the son we would have. He would name him John. He would go on and on about how careful we would be with this child that nothing would happen to this one. He wouldn't entertain the thought of a little girl. I was concerned and I prayed. Please dear God; let us have another son. Ben so needs this Lord. Please God… my prayer … every night…as I grew and grew and grew.

Chapter Twenty Five

I just knew this baby was going to be a big one. I had gained a lot of weight. As we pulled into the hospital parking lot, Ben held my hand tightly with his.

My sister Gail met us at the hospital. It was good seeing her again. She looked radiant. She still was the heaviest of my sisters and in some ways the smartest. She married an engineer of the railroad. He actually was Ben's boss. Hugh was his name. A tall black headed man with a gift of gab. He could talk the paint right off the walls. She had four children, three girls and one boy.

Gail stayed with me throughout my labor. The words I hated to hear came out of the doctor's mouth. Breech. I remembered the horrendous pain that I had with Ethan. NO! I screamed with all my might. At the same time the doctor turned the baby. No pain could be worse than this. My sister took a cool cloth and wiped the beads of sweat from my brow. Finally, it was time for delivery. Gail went out and stayed with Ben in the waiting room. I had gas with this delivery. When I awoke, the nurse smiled at me. She said, "You have a pretty baby girl."

She placed the pink bundle of joy into my arms. She was beautiful. I was happy; however, there was that uneasy feeling in the pit of my stomach. Ben wanted a boy. We had not even discussed the possibility of a girl. Ben was so sure. How would he react to this? She is a part of both of us. She grew out of our love. I dismissed my feelings and decided he would be as happy with her as I was.

The nurse brought Ben and Gail into the room. Gail was instantly picking the beautiful little one up and holding her close. She too had dark hair, though not as dark as Ethan's.

"Guess ya'll are going to have to figure out what to name this sweet girl." she said. Ben walked over to the bed and seemed to force a smile.

"I imagine so," Ben replied. Gail brought the baby around so Ben could see her. "She is very pretty," he replied.

I reached out and took Ben's hand. "We will try again for that son," I said. Ben nodded and remained quiet.

Chapter Twenty Six

Jan was such a good baby. She would sit on the side of the sink while I washed a whole load of dishes, dried them and put them away. She could entertain herself easily and was always ready to take a nap with me. I was always concerned that something would happen to her. I would make sure she ate every bite of food. It wasn't long before Jan was quite a large baby. I had become quite a good cook these past couple years. My home, like my Mama's was spotless. I seemed to have so much nervous energy that I would clean, and then clean again. I remained very thin.

Nothing was ever the same between Ben and me. He would stay out all night long at least once a week and sometimes more. I couldn't sleep and I would just walk the floor. I knew there were two things that would keep Ben out all night. One was gambling and the other was women. If he were not home, I would have to call my brother-n- law Hugh and have him marked off sick. I did not want Ben to lose his position on the railroad. Men were fighting to get these jobs. Times were hard and we just barely managed to keep a roof over our head. Though I would tell myself, if Ben comes home, I will be quiet and not say anything mean to him. However, that did not seem possible with my temper that I inherited from my father.

There were many times Ben gambled and lost. He'd come home and swear he wouldn't gamble anymore. We'd make up and he was gone again…And where was I? Pregnant again.

Oh, I so did not want this baby. I jumped up and down. I drove over bumpy roads. Ben became increasingly distant. He hardly touched me at all. I knew he had another woman. Actually, there were a lot of other women. He was such a handsome man. He never, really was the same after Ethan died. And now, he will not give me the time of day. I'd pace with Jan on my hip and another child in my belly. I had become quite the smoker. I couldn't sleep and I couldn't eat. I could, however, smoke and drink coffee. What had happened to our life together? The love we shared seemed to have soured. Why would God place another child in this womb when he knew good and well Ben is not being a husband to me or a father to Jan?

Jan and I would try to sell Avon. We'd make a little money from the neighbors. I couldn't seem to think my way out of this life and I didn't seem to be able to get Ben to even acknowledge that I was still his wife. All we did was argue, when he was home. I began to wonder if we could still have a life together. Soon we would have another child and then what in the hell would I do?

I took Jan over to Gail's house. I knew I was in labor and someone needed to take me to the hospital. Ben was out somewhere. Gail had her husband Hugh watch the kids and she drove me to the hospital. "I don't want this child Gail," I said. What in the world will I do with another child when Ben doesn't look at the one he has? Gail sat quietly thinking of the right thing to say. She began, "This child is your gift from God to you. Enjoy this child. There is a reason for all things, Aura Leigh."

The doctor gave me a gas mask to use during my labor pains. I would use it when the pain became too intense. The doctor would check on me from time to time and this time, the labor pains did not seem so bad. As my labor advanced, he came in to check on me. Upon entering the room, the doctor stated, "Oh NO! One of them has to go!" I was sitting up on the bed, holding the gas mask in one hand and a cigarette in the other. I had no idea that I could have blown us all up at any moment. Reluctantly, (though cigarettes were held in high regard to me) the cigarette was the one to go…

I had another little girl and named her Dana. I remember thinking she was so small. She resembled a red rat with large ears. She cried a lot. The doctor said she had the colic. I walked and rocked and walked and rocked. She continued to cry. Ben hardly helped at all. He continued to stay gone pretty much. She finally outgrew the colic and by then was spoiled by all the holding. She didn't sit still like Jan. No, she climbed, walked, got into any and everything.

In spite of it all, I loved her. As she grew older, she had sandy blonde hair like Ben. She actually looked quite a lot like Ben and me. She had a sprinkle of freckles across her nose. She was a pretty little girl.

I continued to sell Avon and my route grew. I was making a little money with Jan and Dana by my side. One Saturday, I decided to drive to Flannery with my girls and see my Mama. Ben was not home and I had no clue where he might be. I never knew anymore. Loneliness became a way of life for me and the girls. I had a husband and they had a father, in name only.

On the way to Mama's house, I passed a black mailbox. It had Kurt's name on it. Kurt... How long had it been since I had even had his name cross my mind. What a wonderful boyfriend he was to me growing up. Looking back, I remember the last time I saw Kurt. The last time he held me as I broke up with him. What did he say to me. Those last words echoed in my mind. "Be happy." he had said. Then he walked out of my life. A tear slid down my cheek. What kind of life could I have made for myself and my children with such a man? But, I had not. I had chosen the other road. The more complex road with Ben.

Now, back to reality. Passing the black mailbox slowly, I saw Kurt out in the yard. He was oblivious to me and my car. He was out in the yard playing with children that must be his. He looked the same, though older. His wife was on their porch sitting in a swing. That could've been me in that swing and my children playing with Kurt- Kurt, sweet, sweet Kurt. I had not thought about him in years. He still was so handsome. We were so comfortable together in school, him and me. Had it not been for that train rolling into the station with those camp cars attached, I knew I would have been his wife. Why God? Why did I give up such an easy man for the one I have now? Have now? No, I don't even have him now. I am alone now and a lot of other women have him, one night at a time.

I thought about Virginia. My best friend Virginia... She and Joe were still going strong, so I have heard. Our letter writing and calling had diminished through the years and finally ceased. Though I loved her and always would. I just could not bear for her to see me now. I am sure with Joe working on the railroad he had filled her in on life with Ben. It would be out of respect for me that she would not find me and pry into my business. Though I loved her so and would until the day that I die.

The visit with Mama was nice. She seemed a lot more arthritic as the days have come and gone. She was stooped over now and moving pretty slow. I found out that Leanna and CJ were divorced and Leanna was in the hospital with depression. Mama was attempting to raise Leanna's kids. Time has a way of going so fast, one can hardly keep up with their own life without realizing everyone else's had falling apart. My mother has such strength. I have never known anyone like her, nor will I ever again. After spending the day and enjoying her company I head back home. I don't dare tell Mama about Ben. She has enough on her plate already.

Chapter Twenty Seven

The hot days of summer are here. The back screen door latched and the sounds of the girls playing in the yard echoed up into the kitchen. My wonderful neighbor and now best friend sat at my table sharing cigarettes and a pot of coffee. Her name was Sheila. She had blonde hair and was just beautiful. Her husband was an unfaithful shit to her also. We spent hours at my kitchen table talking about the-what if's and the whys. What a wonderful shoulder she had.

Ben's almost never home anymore. I just try to pretend I have a husband. He'd taken up with only one woman now. It was better when he had many of them. But this one. It's not enough that he stays out with her at night, but the whole town knew. Her name was Margaret. Her husband called and said he would kill Ben…. I don't know, maybe he will, I thought. Ben came home right after the call. "If he said he was going to kill me, then I will die," Ben said. Ben left later that evening and of course did not home. The days rolled on. Margaret's husband soon did die, of what, I am not sure. Margaret was now a single woman…

Ben was like the weather. You never knew what kind of weather you'd have until the next day arrived. He would come in and declare his undying love for me. This might last one, two, or three days… never quite a week. Then he'd be gone for days and days. Margaret had started driving up and down in front of my home with her window rolled down- she would laugh while passing. It's not enough that she pretty much had him, now she wanted to rub it in.

I continue to lose weight. The scales said I weighed less than 90 pounds. I found myself eating dry oatmeal out of the cabinet to fill this gnawing in my stomach. I vomited daily and yelled at my kids. My nights were filled kneeling in my bathroom by the tub. I would wring my hands, pray and call out to God. I would plead and cry. No peace could I find. I couldn't seem to make a firm decision about anything. I would try to sell my Avon. One day my brakes failed while I was delivering my Avon. There was a man and his son walking along the road. I could not stop. What was wrong with my brakes? Did someone tamper with them? It was all so fast. I heard a large thud as I ran over them both. I heard a young boys voice yell, "You killed my daddy, you killed my daddy," over and over I heard this voice. I had hit my head on the steering wheel and had quite a knot on my forehead.

I didn't kill them though I was sure I did. Father and son were hospitalized and after a few weeks they went home ok. I could no longer live in this body with myself. I hated Ben. I couldn't make decisions, and I hated myself. One lonely day, I just couldn't stand living any longer. I took a knife from my kitchen drawer. I would make one decision and do it right. I would die and get out of the way.

Chapter Twenty Eight

Sheila walked in as I was getting ready to end this hellacious life as I knew it. "Leave me alone," I screamed with what strength I could muster. "She grabbed the knife out of my bony little fingers and we sat on the floor. She held me like a child and rocked me soothing me as best as she could. When I calmed down, she called my Mama. I was on my way to the hospital with Ben nowhere in sight.

Sheila dropped my children off at Violet's house. Jan and Dana cried as we pulled away. They had never been away from home and now were going to be staying in another town, another school. My life was not mine anymore. My mind was racing. I felt like the panic would soon consume me and I could go home to live with Jesus and my daddy.

The brick hospital looked extremely clean and orderly as we walked in. I remember little else of that day. I ended up having all the shock treatments a person can have over a series of weeks. The doctor was waiting for me to respond. If not, I would be institutionalized the rest of my days.

I vaguely remember waking up. A lot of my recent memory was gone for good. No memory of my attempted suicide, or a lot of the recent history with Ben. I began talking with this nice doctor. Dr. James was his name. We had daily sessions on how to live. I had two wonderful children and I was young. I was thirty seven and had a full life ahead of me. I had to make quality choices with the rest of my life. His sessions began to give me confidence. Food began to taste good and I started looking forward to mealtime. I ate and I gained my weight back. At 115 pounds I looked and felt much stronger. Mama had been to see me several times and I got better day by day. I wrote to my children and they wrote back to me. Their sweet little letters would come to me almost daily. They seem to be coping well and I cherished the thought of seeing them soon. The girls and I could be a family, even if Ben didn't want to be with us.

Ben did not come to the hospital those six weeks I was there. When I called him to see if he would pick me up at discharge, he said no and sent a taxi that he paid for. While in the hospital, I did receive one card with no name on it. It said, "You would think I would want you to get better." You would think I would, but I don't. It had a witch on the front of the card stirring a large cauldron of brew. I did not let that bother me. I had come through hell and was not going back.

Chapter Twenty Nine

The taxi took me to Violet's house. The children were both in school and her house was quiet. The elementary school that Dana went to was just down the road. I walked about the house and finally made a decision to go to the small school and see if I could pick up Dana. Jan was in the high school and I would need a car to get her. I didn't have a car -at least I can get one of my girls. I walked briskly to the school as excitement of seeing Dana grew.

She was eight years old and in the third grade. I walked into the small two roomed school and saw one of the teachers outside of the classroom. I asked if I could pick Dana up. "Of course you can pick up your little girl" a nice gray haired lady said. I stood by the doorway and looked about the classroom room for her. I saw a little girl with short blonde hair look at me with growing excitement. Could that be her? Did they cut her hair off? The last time Dana saw me, I was skin and bones. Now I weighed 115 pounds. I wasn't sure if the little short haired girl was Dana. She wasn't sure that I was her mother. I had on my red coat that she slowly recognized. Dana slowly got up from her desk and then picked up speed as she came and wrapped her little arms around my waist. She hugged me with all her might. "You are my mother, aren't you?" Dana said. I shook my head yes. Hand in hand we walked back to Violet's. I didn't know what I was going to do, however, now I knew I would do something. The reunion with Jan was wonderful also. She came in from school and there was such a wonderful reunion. Violet made us all a nice dinner. The three of us girls, we would be a family.

Sheila came, picked us up and took us home. Sheila, my friend who saved my life! How grateful I was to this blonde haired wonderful woman! We hugged when she arrived. It was so good to see her. The drive home, we were continuously talking and smoking. It felt so good to be in the car with her. She poured her heart out to me, on the way home. Sheila said she was having an ongoing problem with her husband. She didn't know what she could do. She had four children. How could she possibly go to work?

I walked into my home. It seemed even smaller than its 900sq. feet. No Ben. No sign there was ever a Ben there. All of his clothes were gone. Not even his razor, or his toothbrush was left. Nothing remained, except for one pair of blue and white thin striped coveralls that hung on the line, downstairs in the basement and, in the bedroom, an old wooden box in the chest of drawers. Inside the box were Ben's letters he had sent to me so long ago when we were dating. I had tied them all up with a red ribbon. The pages had yellowed; however, the words still remained.

Sheila had read in the local newspaper of a program. You could get paid for taking business courses. What a blessing I thought. I could get paid while learning a trade. I was excited! I knelt by my bed and prayed for God to please give me this chance to take care of my children.

They accepted me, though I had to put my age back two years. You had to be thirty-five or younger. I was thirty-seven. I decided that I felt like I was thirty-five or maybe even younger. It would not be much of a lie. I enrolled that following Monday. I went to school during the day and I car hopped at night. (Car hops take your order for food at your car and then bring food out to the car when ready.) I was good at it and got a lot of tips. I still was dark and slender. My looks had not faded. That helped. Sometimes guys would get a bit flirty. I certainly wasn't ready for that. I would smile, get my tip and then, walk away.

My girls were so happy to be home. My life was busy and full. I finished up school and got a job at the local bank. I was well liked and I began to climb the ladder of success as the months and years went on. I tried for several years to divorce Ben. He would call and say let's let it ride. I still loved him, however, now I was not foolish enough to die for him. I would take his coveralls down and wash them and hang them back up in my basement each week. This made me feel I still had a part of him with me. Once in a great while, he would pick the kids up for the day. He would look at me and I him. I knew he loved me; however, he could not seem to be able to settle down and come back to me. I knew that I loved him also and would never love another in quite the same way.

Chapter Thirty

I was walking through the local grocery store picking out the weekends food for myself and my girls. Dana so loved hamburgers and coke. While in the vegetable section of the store getting lettuce, I was going over the week's events in my mind. What a busy week this had been with meetings all week at work. I breathed a sigh of relief knowing the weekend was here. I was totally unaware I was being watched.

Hello, a voice said coming from behind me. I turned around and standing there was this black haired man with dark brown eyes. I didn't know him. I was sure of that. I would have remembered those long, dark eyelashes. "I'm new in town," the man went on to say. I am looking for a drive-in movie to take my son to. Someone said it was just down the road a couple miles. Is that right? He asked...

I was a bit startled to say the least. Gaining composure, I said, "Yes, there is a drive in movie theatre a couple miles down on your right." He smiled a nice, friendly smile. I smiled back. "My name is Aura Leigh," I said and extended my hand.

"Mine is John," the stranger said and shook my hand briefly. I stopped for a moment and thought of that name. The same name Ben wanted to name his next son that he never had. I shook the thought out of my mind. How long had it been since I had been attracted to another man. Since the day Ben walked into my life. I was so glad to have this experience and John seemed to be also. He kept standing there thinking of things to say. "Do you come here often," he asked.

"Oh yes," I smiled. This is one of my favorite hangouts, the vegetable aisle at the local supermarket.

I went on to say, "I guess that tells you how exciting my life has become."

"I understand that, it has been a very long time since I have done much of anything." John replied. He said he was divorced and had custody of his son. He also had a business that took a lot of his time. After we talked for twenty minutes or so, we stood there not wanting this moment to end. "Would you like to have a cup of coffee?" John asked.

"I would love to," I said. We loaded our cars with the groceries we had bought and then walked down the street to the local restaurant.

It was easy talking to John. He was a very interesting guy. He had grown up here during his childhood, and then left for the military. He had met and married a young girl from Indiana and had lived there until recently. His divorce had hurt him. I so understood that feeling. After our nice coffee and visit, John walked me to my car. "Can I see you again?" he asked.

"Do you want to meet by the vegetables?" I asked with a smile.

"Why don't I pick you up and we will drive together to the store." "We could finish the evening standing by the milk and cheese," he replied.

I would love that, I said. I gave him directions and a quick hug. He smelled so nice. It was good to have a man hug me again and good to hug him back. Finally, here's a man that I am attracted to. Yeah! I drove home feeling like a teenager again.

The girls were watching television when I arrived home. Instinctively, I gave each girl a big hug. They gave such good hugs.

My home was so neat and clean. Old knotty-pine floors in the bedrooms and living room. There was sunny, yellow linoleum on the kitchen floor. The house was small, but tidy. Jan and Dana shared a room and I had a bedroom to myself. Many nights since Ben left, I would get up and go get Dana out of her bed to sleep with me. It was hard to sleep by myself after all the years with Ben. Dana never fussed about it. She'd just get up and go. A lot of times she didn't even remember getting up and coming to bed with me.

Hamburgers were delicious and the coke was too. After dinner, I called Sheila and asked her to come over and talk awhile. She was right over and I had us a fresh pot of coffee. With the ashtray on the table and smoke rising through the air we talked for hours while the girls played Chinese checkers in the living room floor.

Sheila was thrilled that I actually had a date! It wasn't that I couldn't get a date. I just wouldn't even entertain the idea of dating. I couldn't imagine being with a man that wasn't Ben.

"Aura Leigh, I am so proud of you," Sheila said. "You are finally going to live again." I knew she was right. I had my personal life on hold for such a long time. I felt that I would breathe again. That life would finally go on.

It had been five years since Ben left. I had matured. I had become independent. I had long accepted Ben wouldn't come back to me. He had finally signed the divorce papers. I was a free woman. My emotional scars were healed now and I was ready to begin my new life. I ran downstairs to the basement. I looked at the coveralls that I had washed weekly for years. I took a deep breath and took the clothespins off. The coveralls fell into my arms. I held them close one more time and breathed them in. I folded them and put them in the garbage. It was something I had to do.

Chapter Thirty One

John and I were inseparable. Every spare minute he would come get me. His son and my girls got along very well. He would take us all boating on the lake, or on a picnic and swimming. He always had wonderful plans for us. It wasn't just me. He always included my children also. The kids and I were not used to such adventures. My vacations from the bank meant painting the wall at my house one year, and washing them the next. Other than the drive-in or skating rink, we didn't go out of town. His including my children made me care all the more for him. I was a package deal and so was he. His son was a miniature John. He had black hair, deep brown eyes and long eyelashes also. He was always so polite and giving.

It wasn't long before John and I realized that we loved each other. He was a wonderful kisser and great conversationalist. We could talk all night long and still have something to say the next day.

It was a warm Saturday night when he took me to the local fair. The air was warm and the night was clear. We rode the Ferris wheel. Everything seemed so bright and wonderful. I snuggled next to John as the Ferris wheel descended back towards the ground. My belly felt that light feeling on the way down and we laughed. The next round, Farris wheel stopped. John and I were at the very top. Looking down everything looked so small and insignificant. Johns' eyes were dancing. "What is it?" I asked.

"Aura Leigh, I am so glad that you came into my life and I so want you to become my wife. Will you?" John asked with a smile and a twinkle in those brown eyes.

"I smiled; I'd love to marry you John." He took out a box from his pocket and placed an enormous solitary diamond on my hand. What a ring! It glittered with all the lights shining down on it. I could not have imagined such a ring! With a warm and wonderful kiss, he yelled to the guy operating the machine. "She said yes!" and the Ferris wheel began to move.

Chapter Thirty Two

John and I were quietly married by the justice of the peace. We went to Pigeon Forge, Tennessee, for our honeymoon. It was simple and yet wonderful. We spent our days visiting caverns, and going through stores. Lots of candy shops we would explore. The days were long and lazy. Our nights were warm and romantic. We had a room with a fireplace. I had beautiful nightgowns and he loved them all. He couldn't compliment me enough about my body, my clothes, me. I so needed that and let it all soak in. He was a gentle and wonderful lover. It was different than being with Ben, yet so nice. I loved being a couple, sharing my life once again. I now had a husband that would take good care of me, nurture me and assist me in all I ever hoped to be. I did the same for him. We had learned through life's journeys what was important and what wasn't. We took nothing for granted.

I sold my home and John and I built a beautiful home together. What a house! Mine would have fit inside of it four times! I quit my job and helped him with his business. We worked hard during the days, side by side and at night relaxed with each other. The children grew up and married. They had children of their own. John and I became grand-parents. He loved my grandchildren as much as I did. And I loved his.

It was a comfortable life, like being in a rocking chair. Contentment… It was such a change from the life Ben and I shared. Though the love John and I shared for each other was real and respected, I always had a place in my heart tucked away for Ben. I would take his memory out and enjoy it now and again. I would only think about the first part of our life, our love. Never would I think past Ethan. It was far too painful.

I was happy now. I knew that I found rest with John. I knew he felt the same. Sometimes John was quiet. I figured he had a memory of his first wife tucked away and would enjoy reminiscing periodically also. We never talked about this to one another. We would have both gotten upset. The heart holds its share of secrets.

One day I was pulling out of the bank after my workday was over. An old feeling came back to me. Coming towards me into the bank's parking lot was Ben. He pulled up beside me in my shiny maroon Buick. For a moment, time stood still for us. All the love I had for him tucked away neatly started to rise to the surface. "My God, How beautiful you are Aura Leigh!" Ben said.

"Thank you Ben," I replied softly. "You look kind of tired, Ben." I said.

"I am," he replied. We looked at each other for the longest time, both knowing we would never see each other again. "Are you happy?" Ben asked."

"I am," I said simply. Ben held his hand out the window and I met his hand once again with my own. He hand so firm and so warm. For a moment I felt like I did when leaving Virginia's birthday party so many years ago. I remember running down all those stairs holding onto Ben's hand. It was so warm, so strong. The ride on Ben's bike as he took me home…. his arms about me…..

"I,"—Ben began. He seemed at a loss for words… I looked into Ben's eyes.

"I know," I replied. "I know." He slowly let go of my hand and I realized it was time to move on.

"Be happy too Ben," I said as I began to pull out. He never responded. A wistful look came across Bens' face. I am sure his look mimicked my own.

It was good to see Ben once again. The happiness we once shared ignited again, if, for but a moment….

There is something about letting someone who had hurt you so much realized that you not only survived, but were really living again.

Years and years have gone by since that day. The cemetery where I am placed, by my Mama and my family is atop a fine hill. Surrounding me are the mountains where I grew up and played. Though, I am no longer here, the love that Ben and I once shared will live on in my children and my children's children. And somewhere, in a drawer, tucked away in an old wooden box-tied up in a red ribbon, are those letters now yellowed with the passing of time. They once held so much promise of all the love one would hope for, dreamed of or could have ever imagined and they were mine….

Lightning Source UK Ltd.
Milton Keynes UK
UKHW041537191020
371844UK00002B/472